# The Beach of Falesá

Robert Louis Stevenson

The Beach of Falesá

Edited by Barry Menikoff

Stanford University Press • Stanford, California • 1987

Cover design based on the binding of the Scribners 1893 American
edition of *Island Nights' Entertainments*.

Stanford University Press • Stanford, California
© 1984, 1987 by the Board of Trustees of the
Leland Stanford Junior University
Printed in the United States of America
ISBN 0-8047-1399-5
LC 87-60216
Original printing 1987
Last figure below indicates year of this printing:
98 97 96 95 94 93 92 91 90 89 88 87

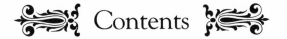 Contents

Introduction, by Barry Menikoff   7
Note on the Text   23

Chapter I. A South Sea Bridal   27
Chapter II. The Ban   39
Chapter III. The Missionary   59
Chapter IV. Devil-Work   70
Chapter V. Night in the Bush   87

Glossary   101

Barry Menikoff

 Introduction

At the time of his forty-fourth birthday, in November 1894, Robert Louis Stevenson enjoyed a celebrity unmatched by any writer of his generation. For nearly a quarter of a century, beginning as a student at the University of Edinburgh, he published poems, articles, and books at a dizzying speed. Stevenson was talented, disciplined, and ambitious for success. He wrote in an extraordinary variety of forms, partly to develop his skills and partly to widen his readership. His early "familiar" essays (*Virginibus Puerisque, Familiar Studies of Men and Books*) revived and modernized a literary form that had gone out of fashion with the passing of the great Romantic essayists. He converted his restlessness into travel literature, creating charming if idiosyncratic books like *Travels with a Donkey* and *The Silverado Squatters*. And of course there was *A Child's Garden of Verses*. Yet even here Stevenson provided a distinctive touch, giving to children's poetry a dimension that went beyond what the child could recognize. He recreated a world of childhood from the vantage point of an adult, a "vanished" world that lived only in the writer's memory and imagination.

But it was not the essays and travel writing and poetry that kept Stevenson's readers spellbound: it was the fiction. From the beginning of his career it was apparent that English fiction had found a new master. The triple decker was still in vogue when Stevenson started to write: "I remember I used to look, in those days, upon every three-volume novel with a sort of veneration, as a feat—not possibly of literature—but at least of physical and moral endurance." Even Henry James questioned the limits of the "old-fashioned English novel," when he confronted the sheer size of *Middlemarch*. Novelists, at least those with artistic impulses, chafed at a system that made bulk writing a condition for publication. Stevenson's response, in both practice and argument, was to alter the customary length of fictional forms. In 1882 he brought out two volumes of his best magazine fiction under the title *New Arabian Nights*. A principal effect of the book was to confer artistic legitimacy on short fiction.

Stevenson's achievement in *New Arabian Nights* was considerable. He was the first major writer to conceive of the short story as a form that threaded together all the technical elements of fiction. Under the guise of entertainment, he introduced serious themes. "The Suicide Club" and "The Rajah's Diamond" offered a picture of contemporary London and Paris that was, beneath the humor and improbable adventures, far from attractive—a picture of life as it was actually experienced, as opposed to life understood through books. In the matter of style, the collection highlighted Stevenson's own dilemma between "romantic story-telling" and writing that was factual, "set forth after the manner of a manual." Further, in the image of the "Rajah's diamond" Stevenson instinctively grasped an idea that was to dominate his thinking and recur in his fiction: the acquisition of treasure and the crimes treasure drives men to commit. But it was "The Pavilion on the Links" that stood out as the centerpiece of the volumes, a story as forceful and vivid as Stevenson was capable of at this time. It was here that he first introduced landscape as a technical device that worked dramatically and symbolically. Although he clearly learned from Poe and Hawthorne, whom he read with concentrated attention, neither of the Americans succeeded in making their settings both realistic *and* symbolic.

Stevenson's self-consciousness about his work was his great strength. From the beginning, his craftsmanship, his experiments with narrative strategies, and his stylistic deliberation set him apart from other writers. But Stevenson was working all this

out in what were essentially popular forms. Perhaps the best ex-
amples are *Treasure Island* and *Strange Case of Dr Jekyll and Mr
Hyde*, the one drawing on the genre of sea stories in the manner
of Marryat and Ballantyne, and the other on the sensational
thriller known as the "penny dreadful" or "shilling shocker."
That *Jekyll and Hyde* was sold in a cheap form in railway book-
stalls, however, did not detract from the quality of the tale. As
for *Treasure Island*, its appearance in a pulp weekly titled *Young
Folks* did not necessarily make it merely a book for the young. In
fact, Stevenson's fidelity to eighteenth-century life in language
and incident (he drew copiously on Daniel Defoe's *General History of the Robberies and Murders of the Most Notorious Pirates*, a
pseudonymous account published in 1724) made *Treasure Island*
a remarkable exercise in historical narrative.

   The truth is that Stevenson used popular forms because they
paid. He was, like Thomas Hardy, a writer caught between the
world of popular fiction, with its large and indiscriminate audience, and the world of the newer serious fiction, with its readership attentive and responsive to artistic issues. He was torn
between his desire to capture a large audience (a desire driven by
his anxiety about money) and his instinctive contempt for this
audience's limited capacity to recognize, let alone to appreciate,
the artistry of his work. Thus the forms of his fiction were not
necessarily illustrative of his intentions; indeed, they were frequently a means of concealment, designed to mask the true
meaning of the work. Just why Stevenson should have gone to
such pains to create in this fashion is beyond the scope of this
Introduction. Suffice it to say that he was ambivalent about the
role of fiction: on the one hand he considered it play for grown-
ups, and on the other an arena for intellectual drama. The "treasure" in his most famous novel, for example, was just another
name for greed, a theme Stevenson could never escape, and one
he returned to later in stories like *The Wrecker* and *The Beach of
Falesá*.

   Following *Treasure Island*, there were further innovations. *Kidnapped* extended the range of Stevenson's fiction to a degree that

was unrecognized for a long time, and *The Master of Ballantrae* experimented with multiple points of view. But even these two books, and particularly *Kidnapped,* presented Stevenson to his audience as a writer of adventure, someone who was at home in his country's past religious and political wars, and a writer whose value resided in his ability to enchant a reader away from reflection and gather him up in the romance of history. By the late 1880's, Stevenson was accordingly in great demand by publishers in England and the United States. Indeed, in January 1892 *The Bookman* placed him second—just behind Rudyard Kipling—on a list of the twelve best-selling British authors.

When Stevenson came to write *The Beach of Falesá,* in 1891, he had been living in Samoa for a year. He had left England in 1887, spent a winter in a tuberculosis sanatorium in upstate New York (during an historic blizzard), and then chartered a yacht in California to set sail for the South Seas. It would be hard to convey the strangeness of Stevenson's undertaking. Although the English had a long tradition of travel and exploration in that part of the globe—Captain Cook was possibly the greatest explorer of the modern world and left a heritage in the South Seas that lasted well into the nineteenth century—nevertheless Pacific travel was not common or casual. The seas could be treacherous. There was no anticipating sudden, heavy squalls. And hydrographers' charts were not altogether dependable. Add to these factors the unreliability of Stevenson's ship (the mast broke in Tahiti, stranding the crew in a remote village) and Stevenson's inclination to visit the most isolated island chains, and the audacity of the venture becomes clearer. What Stevenson discovered on his voyage to windward was a great affinity for the Pacific—for the climate, since it served as a restorative to his health, for the islands, and for their cultures.

Stevenson's initial voyage was made possible by S. S. McClure, a syndicator who contracted with authors to sell their stories to English-language newspapers around the world. McClure agreed to pay Stevenson $10,000 for a series of articles (or "letters") about the South Seas, which would be printed in New York (*The*

Sun) and London (*Black and White*). Stevenson, who disliked writing to a deadline but who liked both the money and the opportunity, accepted the assignment. He started sending back pieces that appeared at weekly intervals during 1890 under the heading "The South Seas." But these descriptive "Letters" were not what the editor at *The Sun* considered appropriate. Stevenson was offering a sophisticated and complex discourse on the culture and history of the islands he visited. Today we would call the genre "ethnohistory" and marvel at Stevenson's prescience. However, what was clear to his contemporaries, to his wife Fanny, and to Sidney Colvin, his literary advisor and confidante, was that the articles were too "scientific"; they were dull and lacked picturesque detail. *The Sun* decided to cancel publication before the completion of the series. Stevenson never had the chance to revise his periodical text (which he viewed as raw material for a major book on the South Seas), and he never saw the book in print. A version was published two years after his death (*In the South Seas*), but, like all of Stevenson's writing during these last years, the text is of questionable reliability, since it was handled by so many different people between manuscript and print stages.

What made the "Letters" so controversial, or perhaps just unpalatable? Put another way, was the issue one of matter or of style? Although the material is classified as "travel literature," it was in an altogether different mode than *Travels with a Donkey*. From a historian's point of view, the material is certainly informative and interesting. Stevenson has frequently been cited as a source in historical studies of the western Pacific, particularly by German scholars. But Stevenson's strategy, both rhetorical and stylistic, was quite original and startling. For one thing, he did not take the stance of the outsider whose own culture was the norm against which the island cultures were judged. Rather, his approach was to discover the indigenous cultures' rationale or operating principles in and of themselves. Thus if cannibalism was a serious issue in the Marquesas (we remember how Melville's narrator was terrified at the prospect of becoming a prisoner of the man-eating Typees), Stevenson wanted to explore the origins of the practice, to speculate on its function, and to determine the attitudes toward the practice held by the Marquesans themselves. This is a signal distance from the assumption that cannibalism was a form of barbarism practiced by people who were, by definition, barbarians.

Further, Stevenson continually made comparisons between the cultures of the Pacific and the history of Europe, as he knew it. Thus the history of Scottish highland clans was regularly juxtaposed with that of Polynesian tribes. This may not seem like much in our own time, but for a late-Victorian writer known for adventure fiction, the approach was considered odd, if not perverse. Additionally—and pointedly—he attributed the devastation of the island populations ("depopulation" was the contemporary term) to the massive diffusion of whites throughout the Pacific. Thus a reader opening his Sunday newspaper in New York might find a long article on how a people who had thrived only fifty years earlier were now all but wiped out. Although there is no way of knowing exactly what readers thought of Stevenson's discourse, the abrupt cancellation of the series, not to mention the criticism leveled at it, suggest that the experience of publication was not a happy one.

Stevenson did not abandon his subject: he merely turned to another, more familiar form for rendering it. Yet the nature of the Pacific material continued to cause problems for him. The story of *The Beach of Falesá* is really two stories, one fictional and the other factual. The factual one was told in my book *Robert Louis Stevenson and 'The Beach of Falesá'* (Stanford, 1984), a story of how Stevenson's text was corrupted in the process of its transmission from manuscript to print. *Falesá* placed Stevenson's friends and business associates in an uncomfortable position. It dealt with issues that editors in London and New York would just as soon not have confronted: issues of language, of sexuality, of race, of politics. What should be clear by now is that by this period Stevenson was determined to write about contemporary life. The fiction that had made him successful (and enabled him to command the prices he did) was not the only fiction he was intent upon writing. There was always a strong element of realism that attached to his work, a function both of his use of place and his particular fidelity to eighteenth-century life. But that was not necessarily what readers, or for that matter critics, took away from his books. For all intents and purposes, Stevenson's work had the mark of a romanticized past written all over it. Given also his compelling style, a style that sang like crystal, it is no wonder that those involved in publishing his fiction preferred the known and comfortable.

But Stevenson's stay in the Pacific was an uncommon experience, and it was inevitable that it would result in an uncommon fiction. Stevenson was not a sojourner in the islands; he was a man who had committed himself to a new life there. If health was a motivating factor, then intellectual interest was a sustaining one: "But the truth is I am committed to the South Seas (where I find everything to interest me and more health than I am used to have) for some time." The Pacific islands offered him a completely new subject, a topographical and cultural territory he could be the first to chart, just as Cook and Krusenstern had mapped the waters before him. It did not mean that he would abandon those themes central to his vision, which he had carried with him from the start of his career; but it did mean that he had a fresh, broad canvas to work upon, which provided him with opportunities he could not have imagined. Stevenson relished the challenge of reproducing in fiction a world of brown women and dispossessed whites, of shipwrecks and tropical foliage, of red sunrises and aquamarine bays. If the setting seemed romantic, the realistic elements in Stevenson's historical novels should have prepared readers for the grim verisimilitude of his first major South Seas fiction.

On the face of it *The Beach of Falesá* has all the elements of a thrilling story—sex, violence, politics, religion, race, and economic exploitation. It is no wonder that Robert McClure, who was syndicating the story for periodical publication, considered it too "strong" as it stood and was convinced that no publisher would print it in Stevenson's original form. But readers today are more likely to recognize the issues in *Falesá* that were hidden or denied by Stevenson's contemporaries. For one thing, we are accustomed to cross-cultural literature, and particularly to literature that derives from the British colonial experience. Kipling, Forster, and Somerset Maugham are among the best-known figures to have worked in this genre. But it was Stevenson who virtually created what Maugham later called the "exotic" short story. With *Falesá* he pointed the way for the next generation, and the next generation would be less inhibited, less bound by Victorian conventions. Yet when all that is taken into account—the acceptance and legitimation of harsher styles of realism, and the willingness to deal with sex and race more openly—it is astonishing how *Falesá* loses nothing by comparison. For Stevenson's story is actually more realistic, possibly even more sexual, than Maugham's classic "Rain." And only Kipling had the knowledge and skill to create as realistic a depiction of cultural differences.

The Beach of Falesá was first published under the title *Uma* in six installments in the *Illustrated London News* (July 2 through August 6, 1892). The story was heavily censored for this initial printing. For example, an early interpolated narrative that formed part of the characterization of Case, the primary force for evil, was eliminated. But the most notorious omission was the cutting of the bogus marriage certificate, the "document" certifying that Wiltshire, the narrator, could take a beautiful island woman for an evening's pleasure and then send her to "hell" the next morning. The first deletion never appeared in print before 1984; the latter became the occasion for all the commentary about Stevenson's problems with the text of *Falesá*. The certificate was restored in the first book publication, although not with the precise wording of the original manuscript.

There was a long gap between the appearance of *Uma* in magazine form and the first book publication, in April 1893, under the title *Island Nights' Entertainments*. The explanation for this delay is complicated. It is sufficient to say here that there were many hands working on the text, at various distances from each other, and often with conflicting motives and interests. Stevenson's friend Sidney Colvin, who acted as a literary advisor and quasi-editor, had little sympathy for the Pacific as a subject and was convinced that he could improve a text that was in its impulse vulgar and perhaps subliterary. Compositors operated on the premise that it was their responsibility to correct and make consistent the punctuation and grammar. Publishers like Scribner's and Cassell were squeamish about language that was a strange mélange of slang and pidgin English, punctuated by obscenities and oaths.

None of these responses to Stevenson's text touches on the substance of the story itself—a story that examined the white man's place in a brown man's culture, that acknowledged a passionate interracial love, and that provided no resolution to either of these issues. In fact, Stevenson made clear that there was no answer to a situation thought to be ugly at worst and tolerable at best. To a culture accustomed to viewing itself as the culmination of civilization (as English culture did), *Falesá* suggested quite the opposite. It would be easy, and not exactly correct, to claim that Stevenson was a critic of late-nineteenth-century imperialism. But he was certainly a critic of the pretensions of European politics—pretensions to doing good, to bringing religion and civilization to benighted peoples.

One of the ways Stevenson put the European position under glass was by forcing the reader to see an Englishman through the eyes of natives. He does this by having the islanders stare at Wiltshire on different occasions. When Wiltshire shows up at church, the preacher looks at him as if he were a strange figure; and the natives sitting around look silently at him as he passes. The effect is to throw Wiltshire off balance: instead of being the central subject, he becomes a central object, the odd man out, stared at and made to feel strange. Stevenson inverts his audience's presumption about who is out of place. If this seems obvious to us, we should remember that the "factual" narratives of eighteenth- and nineteenth-century explorers invariably treated islanders as specimens, often illustrating their volumes with artists' sketches. That Stevenson turns this pattern inside out while retaining the white as his narrator is especially deft: for none of us like to, or rarely even can, see ourselves as exotic in relation to others. This is partly what makes Wiltshire, a bigoted Englishman, such a superb achievement: his moral education is a natural evolution from his situation. As an outsider in a strange land, a man "tabooed" by association, he is forced to see himself as others see him, and in the process to see others differently, perhaps to see them as they are.

And so Stevenson introduced the theme of exile, a theme he went far toward making his own in the last four years of his life. Wiltshire is not an expatriate for political or artistic reasons; nor is he an emigrant searching out a new life in a young country. Rather he is an Englishman living away from home, indeed, one who has no home. But it is not just Wiltshire who is homeless: the island of Falesá is full of exiles thrown together like castaways. Stevenson was intrigued by the whites he met in the Pacific; he wondered how they managed to stay in such alien surroundings. He was struck by their constant talk of going home and his recognition that, like himself, they would never return. Stevenson presents Wiltshire's prototypical exile as a form of imprisonment, relieved only by periodic drinking bouts. He does not address the question of whether the condition of the whites in *Falesá* was a consequence of their isolation and self-exile, or a cause of it. He does, however, reveal them as they are, a class of men that Melville first identified in *Omoo* as "beachcombers," nationless, without commitments or loyalties to any institutions or ideals.

And yet they are not completely without desires or even, on some elementary level, beliefs. Adams, when he is dying, calls out for a priest, a call greeted with cynical derision by Case, which reflects nonetheless Stevenson's view that even the worst men have the rudiments of social impulses. Stevenson never wavered from this belief, a belief that enabled him to write about derelicts with an acknowledgment of their humanity. This does not mean that he saw all men as equally kind or virtuous. But he was aware that good men have a potential for evil, just as evil men have a capacity for generous behavior. This was the substance of *Jekyll and Hyde* and, on a more complex level, of *The Master of Ballantrae*. Stevenson was not fascinated by the idea, so much as convinced that it was a condition of life. This is one reason he admired his performance in creating Wiltshire. He was able to draw a man who exhibited distasteful and sometimes despicable qualities: rough language, racism, chauvinism, exploitation of natives, and a surly, even vicious, attitude toward missionaries. Yet Wiltshire also discloses behavior akin to that of a "gentleman." Stevenson demonstrates how two divergent or perhaps complementary qualities abide in men at the same time. Even Case was kind to his wife, as Wiltshire grudgingly admits; and Mr. Tarleton, at the burial, refuses to acknowledge that Case is unworthy of God's grace. In effect, Stevenson reveals the primary familial and social impulses that even the lowliest of men acknowledge. Wiltshire refers to himself as "a common, low, god-damned white man and British subject, the sort you would like to wipe your boots on." Yet even his self-abasement belies the reality that he strives for something larger, for a recognition that there may be more to life than copra.

And it is in such a recognition that Stevenson introduces the themes of love and sexuality that made *Falesá* so attractive, and uncomfortable, for readers. For one thing, it gave the lie to the notion that Stevenson could not draw women, or write about adult relations. Before *Falesá*, he did not write about women, largely because he did not want to falsify the experience of adult sexuality. Since neither magazine nor book publication allowed for open and candid treatment of sex, Stevenson chose not to treat it at all. But living in Samoa changed that. In "A South Sea Bridal" Uma is described as she first comes out of the water: "She had been fishing; all she wore was a chemise, and it was wetted through, and a cutty sark at that." The clinging shirt heightens Uma's sensuality, and the Scots "cutty sark," with its double meaning of short shift and saucy wench, adds piquancy to the picture. Wiltshire's desire drives him to go along with Case's plan to take Uma as a "wife" in a fake wedding, to be performed in Captain Randall's filthy house. Yet even in this setting Stevenson creates a genuine bridal: Uma "was dressed and scented; her kilt was of fine tapa, looking richer in the folds than any silk; her bust, which was of the colour of dark honey, she wore bare only for some half a dozen necklaces of seeds and flowers; and behind her ears and in her hair, she had the scarlet flowers of the hybiscus." Stunned by Uma's innocence and beauty, Wiltshire's conscience is smitten by the deception played on her. As soon as they leave Captain Randall's house, and are in the "free air," he recognizes that Uma is a "kind of a countess really . . . and no even mate for a poor trader like myself." Uma makes her vow ("Me—your wifie"), and Wiltshire, in one of the book's most striking images, discovers that his sexual desire has been transformed into passionate love: "It had never taken me like that before; but the want of her took and shook all through me, like the wind in the luff of a sail." Stevenson had always been a plain physical sensationist in his prose, and his effort to make the reader experience the physical sensation of love is conveyed in that sentence. Wiltshire's revelation suddenly makes him capable of behavior that he would never have imagined himself capable of. He empties the gin bottles as an avowal of his love for Uma, an act we can only call selfless. Wiltshire's gesture might not be as grand as Merton Densher's renunciation of Milly Theale's money in *The Wings of the Dove*, but the impulse behind it is the same. For Stevenson, as for James, one must give something up to get something of value. And for Uma, accustomed to rough whites, the gesture is a sign of tenderness that she immediately recognizes and responds to.

But if themes like exile and sexuality were unusual for Stevenson, and marked a new development in his fiction, *Falesá*'s technical manipulation of point of view and linguistic experimentation were equally significant achievements. It is a commonplace of Stevenson criticism that he was most successful when using the first person; even more, that the "I" narrators were surrogates for the author, who wrapped himself in his characters to place himself in the action. This is simply untrue. Stevenson was capable of superb fiction in the third person, as *Weir of Hermiston* attests. It *is* true that he felt comfortable with the first-person mode; however, the narrators were not simply personae for the author. This holds for David Balfour as much as for Wiltshire. In the latter Stevenson took considerable pride, for he not only illustrated the kind of man who wound up in the South Pacific ("I'm stuck here"), but a man fashioned out of the region's very language. With the semiliterate Wiltshire, Stevenson could do what Twain had done with Huck Finn: create a literary work from the most unlikely materials. The overriding aim of the experiment was to produce a realistic text that would replicate the world of the South Seas through the eyes and ears of an exiled white trader.

The language of *Falesá*, which embodied that realism, was formed from the "dialects" Stevenson heard and recorded on his travels across the widely scattered islands of the Pacific. It was a bastard idiom, a strange hybrid of sailors' jargon, English and American slang, archaisms that somehow survived, like flotsam, in the speech of traders, and Beach-la-mar, the special language of the region that served as a lingua franca for islanders and whites. Indeed, the title of the novella is a buried reference to this pidgin English that Stevenson believed would one day become the "tongue" of the Pacific. The story was characterized as well by profanity and swearing—Case, for example, could "blaspheme like a Yankee boatswain and talk smut to sicken a kanaka"—an effort on Stevenson's part to be faithful to his material. But it was precisely this aspect of the book that elicited hostility from editors and reviewers—the slang, the profanity, the pidgin, not to mention the "native" diction dispersed like exotica throughout the text. The style, in short, was an affront.

Why did Stevenson work so hard to create a text that was such a departure from his previous writing? For one thing it was a challenge. Stevenson had a great love for languages—he was fluent in Latin and French—and a particular fascination for the coinages that people on the edge of civilization were constantly fabricating. This is what he heard, and he was intent upon its preservation. From the time of its publication, when it was not excoriated for its language, *Falesá* has been identified as a model of the colloquial style in English fiction. It is a style sustained throughout by the idiomatic and expressive voice of the narrator, in which the vernacular is made over into a poetic language. Stevenson's gift for spare, bleak landscape in the Scottish novels becomes, through Wiltshire, a quiet evocation of tropic moons and bright sunrises. The character, Wiltshire, is the voice, but the voice or style is more than the character can understand. For the style itself is one of the beauties of the Pacific. And it is here that Stevenson parted company from his more closed-minded readers: how was it possible, they asked, to create beauty from such ugliness—from derelicts and greed and violence? How can literature be created from such language? The answer of course is that Stevenson's art was ahead of his readers' ability to perceive it, and just at the border of modern fictional realism.

On a fundamental level, the language of *Falesá* functioned as the central theme of the novella. Throughout the text, there are a multiplicity of terms that refer to speech, ranging from descriptive to slangy. And there are countless references to "yarns" and "stories," whose veracity Wiltshire looks upon with skepticism, if not contempt. Why does Stevenson focus so much attention on expression? Clearly the issue is an epistemological one: the more that is said about speech, or the more that assertions are punctuated with "the plain truth" or "it's a fact," then the more we apparently know. Yet the more this is insisted upon, the more we begin to doubt. Wiltshire's entire experience is shrouded in mysteries; he is always thinking or wondering about what is going on, this in spite of the fact that he delivers his narrative retrospectively, after the mysteries have presumably been cleared up. Wiltshire had embarked on a "voyage of discovery" designed to uncover the secret of Case's hold over the islanders and to break Case's monopoly on the copra trade. But Wiltshire's true voyage was one of self-discovery: he is educated into the life of the islands, and out of his bigotry, in spite of himself. It is through language, through his efforts to penetrate the strange and un-yielding dialects, that he tries to come to an understanding of the events on the island of Falesá, and beyond that of his life. Lan-guage is a means of knowing, and knowing is what the novella is about.

Ostensibly there should be no impediment to Wiltshire's ability to find out all he wants to know. The initial obstacle is Wiltshire's ignorance of the "native," which puts him at the mercy of his interpreters. And when Case is the interpreter we feel certain the account is unreliable. On a deeper level, however, all the infor-mation provided to the narrator and presented to the reader comes in the form of interpolated yarns. Case tells Wiltshire stories; Uma tells Wiltshire stories; Tarleton tells Wiltshire sto-ries. And of course Wiltshire tells the reader the enveloping story. These are stories within stories, not quite in the fashion of a Borges ficción, but not far from it. For the truth is (to adopt an expression from Falesá) that not much is learned beyond the de-tails of the plot. The "devil-work" proves a hoax; Case and Wilt-shire have it out in the end, with Case dying and Wiltshire be-coming the sole trader on Falesá; Tarleton prays for Case, and commends his soul, despite Wiltshire's protestations; and Wilt-shire is forced to give the missionary his word that he will not cheat the natives as long as he remains on the island.

But if the ending is satisfying on the level of the plot, it is in other respects completely unsatisfying. The plain truth is that nothing is plain. The queer figures that Wiltshire uses to describe his experience are the counterparts of the "queer figures" that Case constructed to frighten the natives. The basic paradox of Falesá is its use of a realistic and colloquial style, emanating from a plainspoken man, and its inability to draw any absolute conclu-sions from the experience depicted. For the conclusion of the melodrama is not the conclusion of the text; it is merely the end of one of the "yarns" that Wiltshire is relating. The text itself is another yarn, this one without conclusion or resolution. In the final paragraphs of Falesá Wiltshire moves from his main story, which culminated in the death of Case, to the current narrative, after the passage of years. Everyone is accounted for—Black Jack, Randall, Tarleton, even Uma, who is no longer the native beauty of the primary story but a huge Polynesian woman who "could throw a London bobby over her shoulder." Stevenson was quite accurate in his portrayal of islanders, and at the same time unsentimental in completing the picture. From the opening of the novella to the closing, we shift from Uma coming out of the sea to the "old lady" who is giving away the store. Love is not first love, or passionate love, forever.

And then there is Wiltshire himself, father of three children, including two girls. Wiltshire's future is hard to imagine. He himself cannot imagine it. His conscience, or dilemma, is revealed in the portrait of the white racist "stuck" in the islands with "half caste" children, and devoted to them. And how is he to provide for their future? The implicit question is of course how is he to provide for himself? For *The Beach of Falesá* represents a world of shifting structure; it is a text that begins in ambiguity ("I saw that island first when it was neither night nor morning") and ends with a question ("I can't reconcile my mind to their taking up with kanakas, and I'd like to know where I'm to find them whites?"). Just as the slang serves as a form of concealment, to the degree that meaning is mediated, so the meaning of Wiltshire's experience is concealed from him. His dream of a public house in England, a dream even he recognizes as bizarre, is contrasted with the reality of exile on a Pacific island. His "half caste" children are symbols of his divided self, racially and nationally, an idea further figured in the time just before daybreak that serves as a backdrop for the chapters. For Wiltshire as for the reader, language is an instrument of great suppleness and ultimate bafflement, just as life is a mixture of passionate vitality and final disappointment. Stevenson, by folding his smaller "yarns" within his larger tale, created a layered text, without resolution for either character or reader, a text for the modern age.

Note on the Text

The text of *Falesá* is that of the holograph fair-copy manuscript. My intention has been to preserve the accidentals as faithfully as possible. However, a number of emendations have been made. The spelling of *niether*, *nieghbour*, *wieghed*, and *siezed* has been regularized, and *Christmass*, *breach*, *sorceror*, *obeissance*, *parasytes*, and *Blavattsky* are printed *Christmas*, *breech*, *sorcerer*, *obeisance*, *parasites*, and *Blavatsky*. Further, the compounds *underway*, *backroom*, *anyman*, and *ill-will* have been separated, and *rëassured* is printed without the diacritical mark. Where Stevenson alternated *Johnny* and *Johnnie* for the same character, the first form has been adopted. Apostrophes have been added to *it's* (three times), *hour's*, *that's*, and *wives'*; *mechanic's* and *mens'* are corrected to *mechanics'* and *men's*; and *aitu's* and *kanaka's* are changed to *aitus* and *kanakas*. Stevenson alternated between *aint* and *ain't*, and the latter form has been adopted. *Monday* has the initial letter capitalized; *Randall* has the second *l* added on two occasions; double quotation marks are added in two cases, and single quotation marks are substituted for double quotation marks in four cases; and terminal periods have been supplied for sixteen sentences. The words *Case*, *part*, and *to* have been added to the text, along with the alteration of *I'* to *I've* and *We'll* to *Well*. These emendations, with the exceptions of making consistent the spelling of *Johnny* and the deletion of the hyphen from *ill-will*, appear in all the printed texts from the galley proofs to the American edition published by Scribner's.

Stevenson's few lapses from consistency are noted: *Papa-Mālūlū*, emended only in the *Illustrated London News* text to *Papa-mālūlū*, is printed here with the lowercase *m*, in conformity with Stevenson's practice throughout *Falesá*; *lord* is raised to *Lord* in one case, and *Papa* reduced to *papa* in another. *Fale-alii* and *mummy-apples*, again in accordance with Stevenson's practice, have hyphens added. Stevenson's inconsistent hyphenation of *Hard shell* and *hard-shell* has been retained, as well as his alternate writing of *Faavao* and *Fa'avao*. Additionally, in one place *to*, deleted from all previous texts, is emended here to *too*, and an *a* has been supplied where it does not appear in the manuscript.

The more critical question of Stevenson's corrections for the "Bottle Imp" edition proved less difficult than one might have expected. The great majority of his revisions simply restored the punctuation and language of the manuscript. In eleven instances, however, he made changes from the manuscript punctuation. But in these cases he was working with repunctuated or corrupted sentences, so the holograph punctuation has been retained. Stevenson also made three changes where the punctuation was printed correctly: two semicolons were altered to dashes, and an exclamation mark was substituted for a comma. These have been incorporated in this edition. Finally, Stevenson made three changes in wording: *spun* became *span*, *talo pepelo* was corrected to *tala pepelo*, and *since* was changed to *even if*. These revisions have also been incorporated. In cases where the manuscript is illegible or unclear, I have followed the Cassell edition.

A Glossary explaining a number of Stevenson's less obvious slang and nautical terms follows the text.

The Beach of Falesá

To Three Old Shipmates among the Islands

Harry Henderson
Ben Hird
Jack Buckland

Their Friend
R.L.S.

Chapter I

 # A South Sea Bridal

I saw that island first when it was neither night nor morning. The moon was to the west, setting but still broad and bright. To the east, and right amidships of the dawn, which was all pink, the daystar sparkled like a diamond. The land breeze blew in our faces and smelt strong of wild lime and vanilla: other things besides, but these were the most plain; and the chill of it set me sneezing. I should say I had been for years on a low island near the line, living for the most part solitary among natives. Here was a fresh experience; even the tongue would be quite strange to me; and the look of these woods and mountains, and the rare smell of them, renewed my blood.

The captain blew out the binnacle lamp.

"There," said he, "there goes a bit of smoke, Mr Wiltshire, behind the break of the reef. That's Falesá where your station is, the last village to the east; nobody lives to windward, I don't know why. Take my glass, and you can make the houses out."

I took the glass; and the shores leaped nearer, and I saw the tangle of the woods and the breach of the surf, and the brown roofs and the black insides of houses peeped among the trees.

"Do you catch a bit of white there to the east'ard?" the captain continued. "That's your house. Coral built, stands high, verandah you could walk on three abreast: best station in the South Pacific. When old Adams saw it, he took and shook me by the hand.—'I've dropped into a soft thing here,' says he.—'So you have,' says I, 'and time too!' Poor Johnny! I never saw him again but the once,

and then he had changed his tune—couldn't get on with the natives, or the whites, or something; and the next time we came
round, there he was dead and buried. I took and put up a bit of a
stick to him: 'John Adams, *obit* eighteen and sixty eight. Go thou
and do likewise.' I missed that man; I never could see much harm
in Johnny."

"What did he die of?" I inquired.

"Some kind of a sickness," says the captain. "It appears it took
him sudden. Seems he got up in the night, and filled up on Pain-
Killer and Kennedy's Discovery: no go—he was booked beyond
Kennedy. Then he had tried to open a case of gin; no go again—
not strong enough. Then he must have turned to and run out on
the verandah, and capsized over the rail. When they found him
the next day, he was clean crazy—carried on all the time about
somebody watering his copra. Poor John!"

"Was it thought to be the island?" I asked.

"Well, it was thought to be the island, or the trouble, or something," he replied. "I never could hear but what it was a healthy
place. Our last man, Vigours, never turned a hair. He left because
of the beach; said he was afraid of Black Jack and Case and Whistling Jimmie, who was still alive at the time but got drowned soon
afterward when drunk. As for old Captain Randall, he's been here
any time since eighteen forty, forty five. I never could see much
harm in Billy, nor much change. Seems as if he might live to be
old Kafoozleum. No, I guess its healthy."

"There's a boat coming now," said I. "She's right in the pass;
looks to be a sixteen foot whale; two white men in the stern
sheets."

"That's the boat that drowned Whistling Jimmie!" cried the
captain. "Let's see the glass. Yes: that's Case, sure enough, and the
darkie. They've got a gallows bad reputation, but you know what
a place the beach is for talking. My belief, that Whistling Jimmie
was the worst of the trouble; and he's gone to glory, you see.
What'll you bet they ain't after gin? Lay you five to two they take
six cases."

When these two traders came aboard I was pleased with the

looks of them at once; or rather, with the looks of both, and the speech of one. I was sick for white neighbours after my four years at the line, which I always counted years of prison; getting tabooed, and going down to the Speak House to see and get it taken off; buying gin, and going on a break, and then repenting; sitting in my house at night with the lamp for company; or walking on the beach and wondering what kind of a fool to call myself for being where I was. There were no other whites upon my island; and when I sailed to the next, rough customers made the most of the society. Now to see these two when they came aboard, was a pleasure. One was a negro to be sure; but they were both rigged out smart in striped pyjamas and straw hats, and Case would have passed muster in a city. He was yellow and smallish; had a hawk's nose to his face, pale eyes, and his beard trimmed with scissors. No man knew his country, beyond he was of English speech; and it was clear he came of a good family and was splendidly educated. He was accomplished too; played the accordion first rate; and give him a piece of string or a cork or a pack of cards, and he could show you tricks equal to any professional. He could speak when he chose fit for a drawing room; and when he chose he could blaspheme worse than a Yankee boatswain and talk smut to sicken a kanaka. The way he thought would pay best at the moment, that was Case's way; and it always seemed to come natural and like as if he was born to it. He had the courage of a lion and the cunning of a rat; and if he's not in Hell today, there's no such place. I know but one good point to the man; that he was fond of his wife and kind to her. She was a Sāmoa woman, and dyed her hair red, Sāmoa style; and when he came to die (as I have to tell of) they found one strange thing, that he had made a will like a christian and the widow got the lot. All his, they said, and all Black Jack's, and the most of Billy Randall's in the bargain; for it was Case that kept the books. So she went off home in the schooner *Manu'a*, and does the lady to this day in her own place.

But of all this, on that first morning, I knew no more than a fly. Case used me like a gentleman and like a friend, made me welcome to Falesá, and put his services at my disposal, which was the more helpful from my ignorance of the native. All the early part of the day, we sat drinking better acquaintance in the cabin, and I never heard a man talk more to the point. There was no smarter trader, and none dodgier, in the islands. I remember one bit of advice he gave that morning, and one yarn he told. The bit of advice was this. "Whenever you get hold of any money," says he—"any christian money, I mean—the first thing to do is to fire it up to Sydney to the bank. It's only a temptation to a copra merchant; some day, he'll be in a row with the other traders, and he'll get his shirt out and buy copra with it. And the name of the man that buys copra with gold is Damfool," says he. That was the advice; and this was the yarn, which might have opened my eyes to the danger of that man for a neighbour, if I had been anyway suspicious. It seems Case was trading somewhere in the Ellices. There was a man Miller a Dutchman there, who had a strong hold with the natives and handled the bulk of what there was. Well one fine day a schooner got wrecked in the lagoon, and Miller bought her (the way these things are usually managed) for an old song, which was the ruin of him. For having a lot of trade on hand that had cost him practically nothing, what does he do but begin cutting rates? Case went round to the other traders. "Wants to lower prices?" says Case. "All right, then. He has five times the turn-over of any one of us; if buying at a loss is the game, he stands to lose five times more. Let's give him the bed rock; let's bilge the ———!" And so they did, and five months after, Miller had to sell out his boat and station, and begin again somewhere in the Carolines.

All this talk suited me, and my new companion suited me, and I thought Falesá seemed to be the right kind of a place; and the more I drank, the lighter my heart. Our last trader had fled the place at half an hour's notice, taking a chance passage in a labour ship from up west; the captain, when he came, had found the station closed, the keys left with the native pastor, and a letter from the runaway confessing he was fairly frightened of his life. Since then the firm had not been represented and of course there was no cargo; the wind besides was fair, the captain hoped he could make his next island by dawn, with a good tide; and the business of landing my trade was gone about lively. There was no call for me to fool with it, Case said; nobody would touch my things, everyone was honest in Falesá, only about chickens or an odd knife or an odd stick of tobacco; and the best I could do was to sit quiet till the vessel left, then come straight to his house, see old Captain Randall, the father of the Beach, take pot luck, and go home to sleep when it got dark. So it was high noon, and the schooner was under way, before I set my foot on shore at Falesá.

I had a glass or two on board, I was just off a long cruise and the ground heaved under me like a ship's deck. The world was like all new painted; my foot went along to music; Falesá might have been Fiddler's Green, if there is such a place, and more's the pity if there isn't! It was good to foot the grass, to look aloft at the green mountains, to see the men with their green wreaths and the women in their bright dresses, red and blue. On we went, in the strong sun and the cool shadow, liking both; and all the children in the town came trotting after with their shaven heads and their brown bodies, and raising a thin kind of a cheer in our wake, like crowing poultry.

"By the by," says Case, "we must get you a wife."

"That's so," said I, "I had forgotten."

There was a crowd of girls about us, and I pulled myself up and looked among them like a Bashaw. They were all dressed out for the sake of the ship being in; and the women of Falesá are a handsome lot to see. If they have a fault, they are a trifle broad in the beam; and I was just thinking so when Case touched me.

"That's pretty," says he.

I saw one coming on the other side alone. She had been fishing; all she wore was a chemise, and it was wetted through, and a cutty sark at that. She was young and very slender for an island maid, with a long face, a high forehead, and a sly, strange, blindish look between a cat's and a baby's.

"Who's she?" said I. "She'll do."

"That's Uma," said Case, and he called her up and spoke to her in the native. I didn't know what he said; but when he was in the midst, she looked up at me quick and timid like a child dodging a blow; then down again; and presently smiled. She had a wide mouth, the lips and the chin cut like any statue's; and the smile came out for a moment and was gone. There she stood with her head bent and heard Case to an end; spoke back in the pretty Polynesian voice, looking him full in the face; heard him again in answer; and then with an obeisance started off. I had just a share of the bow, but never another shot of her eye; and there was no more word of smiling.

"I guess it's all right," said Case. "I guess you can have her. I'll make it square with the old lady. You can have your pick of the lot for a plug of tobacco," he added, sneering.

I suppose it was the smile stuck in my memory, for I spoke back sharp. "She doesn't look that sort," I cried.

"I don't know that she is," said Case. "I believe she's as right as the mail. Keeps to herself, don't go round with the gang, and that. O, no, don't you misunderstand me—Uma's on the square." He spoke eager I thought, and that surprised and pleased me. "Indeed," he went on, "I shouldn't make so sure of getting her, only she cottoned to the cut of your jib. All you have to do is to keep dark and let me work the mother my own way; and I'll bring the girl round to the captain's for the marriage."

I didn't care for the word marriage, and I said so.

"O, there's nothing to hurt in the marriage," says he. "Black Jack's the chaplain."

By this time we had come in view of the house of these three white men; for a negro is counted a white man—and so is a Chinese! a strange idea, but common in the islands. It was a board house with a strip of ricketty verandah. The store was to the front, with a counter, scales and the poorest possible display of trade: a case or two of tinned meats; a barrel of hard bread; a few bolts of cotton stuff, not to be compared with mine; the only thing well represented being the contraband—fire arms and liquor. "If these are my only rivals," thinks I, "I should do well in Falesá." Indeed there was only the one way they could touch me, and that was with the guns and drink.

In the back room was old Captain Randall, squatting on the

floor native fashion, fat and pale, naked to the waist, gray as a badger and his eyes set with drink. His body was covered with gray hair and crawled over by flies; one was in the corner of his eye— he never heeded; and the mosquitoes hummed about the man like bees. Any clean-minded man would have had the creature out at once and buried him; and to see him, and think he was seventy, and remember he had once commanded a ship, and come ashore in his smart togs, and talked big in bars and consulates, and sat in club verandahs, turned me sick and sober.

He tried to get up when I came in, but that was hopeless; so he reached me a hand instead and stumbled out some salutation.

"Papa's pretty full this morning," observed Case. "We've had an epidemic here; and Captain Randall takes gin for a prophylactic— don't you, papa?"

"Never took such thing my life!" cried the captain, indignantly. "Take gin for my health's sake, Mr Wha's-ever-your-name. 'S a precaution'ry measure."

"That's all right, papa," said Case. "But you'll have to brace up. There's going to be a marriage, Mr Wiltshire here is going to get spliced."

The old man asked to whom.

"To Uma," said Case.

"Uma?" cried the captain. "Wha's he want Uma for? 'S he come here for his health, anyway? Wha' 'n hell's he want Uma for?"

"Dry up papa," said Case. " 'Tain't you that's to marry her. I guess you're not her godfather and godmother; I guess Mr Wiltshire's going to please himself."

With that he made an excuse to me that he must move about the marriage, and left me alone with the poor wretch that was his partner and (to speak truth) his gull. Trade and station belonged both to Randall; Case and the negro were parasites; they crawled and fed upon him like the flies, he none the wiser. Indeed I have no harm to say of Billy Randall, beyond the fact that my gorge rose at him, and the time I now passed in his company was like a nightmare.

The room was stifling hot and full of flies; for the house was dirty and low and small, and stood in a bad place, behind the village, in the borders of the bush, and sheltered from the trade. The three men's beds were on the floor, and a litter of pans and dishes. There was no standing furniture, Randall, when he was violent, tearing it to laths. There I sat, and had a meal which was served us by Case's wife; and there I was entertained all day by that remains of man, his tongue stumbling among low old jokes and long old stories, and his own wheezy laughter always ready, so that he had no sense of my depression. He was nipping gin all the while; sometimes he fell asleep and awoke again whimpering and shivering; and every now and again he would ask me why in Hell I wanted to marry Uma. "My friend," I was telling myself all day, "you must not be an old gentleman like this."

It might be four in the afternoon perhaps, when the backdoor was thrust slowly open, and a strange old native woman crawled into the house almost on her belly. She was swathed in black stuff to her heels; her hair was gray in swatches; her face was tattooed, which was not the practise in that island; her eyes big and bright and crazy. These she fixed upon me with a wrapt expression that I saw to be part acting; she said no plain word, but smacked and mumbled with her lips, and hummed aloud, like a child over its Christmas pudding. She came straight across the house heading for me, and as soon as she was alongside, caught up my hand and purred and crooned over it like a great cat. From this she slipped into a kind of song.

"Who in the devil's this?" cried I, for the thing startled me.

"It's Faavao," says Randall, and I saw he had hitched along the floor into the farthest corner.

"You ain't afraid of her?" I cried.

"Me 'fraid!" cried the captain. "My dear friend, I defy her! I don't let her put her foot in here. Only I suppose 's diff'ent today for the marriage. 'S Uma's mother."

"Well, suppose it is, what's she carrying on about?" I asked, more irritated, perhaps more frightened than I cared to show; and the captain told me she was making up a quantity of poetry in my praise because I was to marry Uma. "All right, old lady," says I, with rather a failure of a laugh. "Anything to oblige. But when you're done with my hand, you might let me know."

She did as though she understood; the song rose into a cry and stopped; the woman crouched out of the house the same way that she came in, and must have plunged straight into the bush, for when I followed her to the door she had already vanished.

"These are rum manners," said I.

" 'S a rum crowd," said the captain, and to my surprise he made the sign of the cross on his bare bosom.

"Hillo!" says I, "are you a papist?"

He repudiated the idea with contempt. "Hard-shell Baptis'," said he. "But, my dear friend, the papists got some good ideas too; and tha' 's one of 'em. You take my advice, and whenever you come across Uma or Faavao or Vigours or any of that crowd, you take a leaf out o' the priests, and do what I do: savvy?" says he, repeated the sign, and winked his dim eye at me. "No, *sir!*" he broke out again, "no papists here!" and for a long time entertained me with his religious opinions.

I must have been taken with Uma from the first, or I should certainly have fled from that house and got into the clean air, and the clean sea or some convenient river. Though it's true I was committed to Case; and besides I could never have held my head up in that island, if I had run from a girl upon my wedding night.

The sun was down, the sky all on fire and the lamp had been sometime lighted, when Case came back with Uma and the negro. She was dressed and scented; her kilt was of fine tapa, looking richer in the folds than any silk; her bust, which was of the colour of dark honey, she wore bare only for some half a dozen necklaces of seeds and flowers; and behind her ears and in her hair, she had the scarlet flowers of the hybiscus. She showed the best bearing for a bride conceivable, serious and still; and I thought shame to stand up with her in that mean house and before that grinning negro. I thought shame I say; for the mountebank was dressed with a big paper collar, the book he made believe to read from was an odd volume of a novel, and the words of his service not fit to be set down. My conscience smote me when we joined hands; and when she got her certificate, I was tempted to throw up the bargain and confess. Here is the document: it was Case that wrote it, signatures and all, in a leaf out of the ledger.

This is to certify that _Uma_ daughter of _Faavao_ of Falesá island of ————, is illegally married to Mr John Wiltshire for one night, and Mr John Wiltshire is at liberty to send her to hell next morning.

John Blackamoor
Chaplain to the Hulks.

Extracted from the register
  by William T. Randall
    Master Mariner.

That was a nice paper to put in a girl's hand and see her hide away like gold. A man might easily feel cheap for less. But it was the practise in these parts, and (as I told myself) not the least the fault of us White Men but of the missionaries. If they had let the natives be, I had never needed this deception, but taken all the wives I wished, and left them when I pleased, with a clear conscience.

The more ashamed I was, the more hurry I was in to be gone; and our desires thus jumping together, I made the less remark of a change in the traders. Case had been all eagerness to keep me; now, as though he had attained a purpose, he seemed all eagerness to have me go. Uma, he said, could show me to my house, and the three bade us farewell indoors.

The night was nearly come; the village smellt of trees, and flowers and the sea, and breadfruit cooking; there came a fine roll of sea from the reef, and from a distance, among the woods and houses, many pretty sounds of men and children. It did me good to breathe free air; it did me good to be done with the captain and see, instead, the creature at my side. I felt for all the world as though she were some girl at home in the old country, and forgetting myself for the minute, took her hand to walk with. Her fingers nestled into mine; I heard her breathe deep and quick; and all at once she caught my hand to her face and pressed it there. "You good!" she cried, and ran ahead of me, and stopped and looked back and smiled, and ran ahead of me again; thus guiding me through the edge of the bush and by a quiet way to my own house.

The truth is Case had done the courting for me in style; told her I was mad to have her and cared nothing for the consequence; and the poor soul, knowing that which I was still ignorant of, believed it every word, and had her head nigh turned with vanity and gratitude. Now of all this I had no guess; I was one of those most opposed to any nonsense about native women, having seen so many whites eaten up by their wives' relatives and made fools of in the bargain; and I told myself I must make a stand at once and bring her to her bearings. But she looked so quaint and pretty as she ran away and then awaited me, and the thing was done so like a child or a kind dog, that the best I could do was just to follow her whenever she went on, to listen for the fall of her bare feet, and to watch in the dusk for the shining of her body. And there was another thought came in my head. She played kitten with me now when we were alone; but in the house she had carried it the way a countess might, so proud and humble. And what with her dress—for all there was so little of it, and that native enough—what with her fine tapa and fine scents, and her red flowers and seeds that were quite as bright as jewels, only larger—it came over me she was a kind of a countess really, dressed to hear great singers at a concert, and no even mate for a poor trader like myself.

She was the first in the house; and while I was still without, I saw a match flash and the lamplight kindle in the windows. The station was a wonderful fine place, coral built, with quite a wide verandah, and the main room high and wide. My chests and cases had been piled in, and made rather of a mess; and there, in the thick of the confusion, stood Uma by the table, awaiting me. Her shadow went all the way up behind her into the hollow of the iron roof; she stood against it bright, the lamplight shining on her skin. I stopped in the door, and she looked at me, not speaking, with eyes that were eager and yet daunted. Then she touched herself on the bosom. "Me—your wifie," she said. It had never taken me like that before; but the want of her took and shook all through me, like the wind in the luff of a sail.

I could not speak, if I had wanted; and if I could, I would not. I was ashamed to be so much moved about a native; ashamed of the marriage too, and the certificate she had treasured in her kilt; and I turned aside and made believe to rummage among my cases. The first thing I lighted on was a case of gin, the only one that I had brought; and partly for the girl's sake, and partly for horror of the recollection of old Randall, took a sudden resolve. I prized the lid off; one by one, I drew the bottles with a pocket corkscrew, and sent Uma out to pour the stuff from the verandah.

She came back after the last, and looked at me puzzled like.

"Why you do that?" she asked.

"No good," said I, for I was now a little better master of my tongue. "Man he drink, he no good."

She agreed with this but kept considering. "Why you bring him?" she asked presently. "Suppose you no want drink, you no bring him, I think."

"That's all right," said I. "One time I want drink too much; now no want. You see I no savvy I get one little wifie. Suppose I drink gin, my little wifie he 'fraid."

To speak to her kindly was about more than I was fit for; I had made my vow I would never let on to weakness with a native; and I had nothing for it but to stop.

She stood looking gravely down at me where I sat by the open case. "I think you good man," she said. And suddenly she had fallen before me on the floor. "I belong you all-e-same pig!" she cried.

Chapter II

 # The Ban

I came on the verandah just before the sun rose on the morrow. My house was the last on the east; there was a cape of woods and cliffs behind that hid the sunrise. To the west, a swift cold river ran down, and beyond was the green of the village, dotted with cocoapalms and breadfruits and houses. The shutters were some of them down and some open; I saw the mosquito bars still stretched, with shadows of people new wakened sitting up inside; and all over the green others were stalking silent, wrapped in their many-coloured sleeping clothes like Bedouins in bible pictures. It was mortal still and solemn and chilly; and the light of the dawn on the lagoon was like the shining of a fire.

But the thing that troubled me was nearer hand. Some dozen young men and children made a piece of a half circle, flanking my house; the river divided them, some were on the near side, some on the far, and one on a boulder in the midst; and they all sat silent, wrapped in their sheets, and stared at me and my house as straight as pointer dogs. I thought it strange as I went out. When I had bathed and come back again, and found them all there, and two or three more along with them, I thought it stranger still. What could they see to gaze at in my house? I wondered, and went in.

But the thought of these starers stuck in my mind, and presently I came out again. The sun was now up, but it was still behind the cape of woods: say quarter of an hour had come and gone. The crowd was greatly increased, the far bank of the river was lined for quite a way; perhaps thirty grown folk, and of children twice as many, some standing, some squatted on the ground, and all staring at my house. I have seen a house in a South Sea village thus surrounded, but then a trader was thrashing his wife inside, and she singing out. Here was nothing: the stove was alight, the smoke going up in a Christian manner; all was shipshape and Bristol fashion. To be sure, there was a stranger come; but they had a chance to see that stranger yesterday and took it quiet enough. What ailed them now? I leaned my arms on the rail and stared back. Devil a wink they had in them. Now and then I could see the children chatter, but they spoke so low not even the hum of their speaking came my length. The rest were like graven images; they stared at me, dumb and sorrowful, with their bright eyes; and it came upon me things would look not much different, if I were on the platform of the gallows, and these good folk had come to see me hanged.

I felt I was getting daunted, and began to be afraid I looked it, which would never do. Up I stood, made believe to stretch myself, came down the verandah stair, and strolled towards the river. There went a short buzz from one to the other, like what you hear in theatres when the curtain goes up; and some of the nearest gave back the matter of a pace. I saw a girl lay one hand on a young man and make a gesture upward with the other; at the same time she said something in the native with a gasping voice. Three little boys sat beside my path, where I must pass within three feet of them. Wrapped in their sheets, with their shaved heads and bits of top-knots, and queer faces, they looked like figures on a chimney piece. Awhile they sat their ground, solemn as judges; I came up hand over fist, doing my five knots, like a man that meant business; and I thought I saw a sort of a wink and gulp in the three faces. Then one jumped up (he was the farthest off) and ran for his mammy. The other two, trying to follow suit, got foul, came to ground together bawling, wriggled right out of their sheets—and in a moment there were all three of them, two mother naked, scampering for their lives and singing out like pigs. The natives, who would never let a joke slip even at a burial, laughed and let up, as short as a dog's bark.

They say it scares a man to be alone. No such thing. What scares him in the dark or the high bush, is that he can't make sure, and there might be an army at his elbow. What scares him worst is to be right in the midst of a crowd, and have no guess of what they're driving at. When that laugh stopped, I stopped too. The boys had not yet made their offing; they were still on the full stretch going the one way, when I had already gone about ship and was sheering off the other. Like a fool I had come out, doing my five knots; like a fool I went back again. It must have been the funniest thing to see; and what knocked me silly, this time no one laughed; only one old woman gave a kind of pious moan, the way you have heard dissenters in their chapels at the sermon.

"I never saw such damfool kanakas as your people here," I said once to Uma, glancing out of the window at the starers.

"Savvy nothing," says Uma, with a kind of a disgusted air that she was good at.

And that was all the talk we had upon the matter; for I was put out, and Uma took the thing so much as a matter of course, that I was fairly ashamed.

All day, off and on, now fewer and now more, the fools sat about the west end of my house and across the river, waiting for the show, whatever that was—fire to come down from heaven, I suppose, and consume me bones and baggage. But by evening, like real islanders, they had wearied of the business; and got away and had a dance instead in the big house of the village, where I heard them singing and clapping hands till maybe ten at night; and the next day, it seemed they had forgotten I existed. If fire had come down from heaven or the earth opened and swallowed me, there would have been nobody to see the sport or take the lesson, or whatever you like to call it. But I was to find they hadn't forgot either, and kept an eye lifting for phenomena over my way.

I was hard at it both these days getting my trade in order, and taking stock of what Vigours had left. This was a job that made me pretty sick, and kept me from thinking on much else. Ben had taken stock the trip before, I knew I could trust Ben; but it was plain somebody had been making free in the meantime. I found I was out by what might easy cover six months salary and profit; and

I could have kicked myself all round the village to have been such a blamed ass, sitting boozing with that Case, instead of attending to my own affairs and taking stock.

However, there's no use crying over spilt milk. It was done now and couldn't be undone. All I could do was to get what was left of it, and my new stuff (my own choice) in order, to go round and get after the rats and cockroaches, and to fix up that store regular Sydney style. A fine show I made of it; and the third morning, when I had lit my pipe and stood in the doorway and looked in— and turned and looked far up the mountain, and saw the cocoanuts waving, and footed up the tons of copra—and over the village green and saw the island dandies, and reckoned up the yards of print they wanted for their kilts and dresses—I felt as if I was in the right place to make a fortune, and go home again, and start a public house. There was I sitting in that verandah, in as handsome a piece of scenery as you could find, a splendid sun, and a fine, fresh healthy trade that stirred up a man's blood like seabathing; and the whole thing was clean gone from me, and I was dreaming England, which is after all a nasty, cold, muddy hole, with not enough light to see to read by—and dreaming the looks of my public, by a kant of a broad highroad like an avenue and with the sign on a green tree.

So much for the morning, but the day passed and the devil any one looked near me, and from all I knew of natives in other islands, I thought this strange. People laughed a little at our firm, and their fine stations, and at this station of Falesá in particular: all the copra in the district wouldn't pay for it (I had heard them say) in fifty years; which I supposed was an exaggeration. But when the day went and no business came at all, I began to get down-hearted, and about three in the afternoon, I went out for a stroll to cheer me up. On the green I saw a white man coming with a cassock on, by which and by the face of him, I knew he was a priest. He was a good natured old soul to look at, gone a little grizzled, and so dirty you could have written with him on a piece of paper.

"Good day, sir," says I.

He answered me eagerly in native.

"Don't you speak any English?" said I.

"Franch," says he.

"Well," said I, "I'm sorry, but I can't do anything there."

He tried me awhile in the French, and then again in native, which he seemed to think was the best chance. I made out he was after more than passing the time of day with me, but had something to communicate, and I listened the harder. I heard the names of Adams and Case and of Randall—Randall the oftenest; and the word "poison" or something like it; and a native word that he said very often. I went home repeating it to myself.

"What does *fussy-ocky* mean?" I asked of Uma, for that was as near as I could come to it.

"Make dead," said she.

"The devil it does!" says I. "Did ever you hear that Case had poisoned Johnny Adams?"

"Every man he savvy that," says Uma, scornful like. "Give him white sand—bad sand. He got the bottle still. Suppose he give you gin, you no take him."

Now I had heard much the same sort of story in other islands, and the same white powder always to the front, which made me think the less of it. For all that I went over to Randall's place, to see what I could pick up, and found Case on the door step cleaning a gun.

"Good shooting here?" says I.

"A one," says he. "The bush is full of all kinds of birds. I wish copra was as plenty," says he, I thought slyly, "but there don't seem anything doing."

I could see Black Jack in the store serving a customer.

"That looks like business, though," said I.

"That's the first sale we've made in three weeks," said he.

"You don't tell me?" says I. "Three weeks? Well, well."

"If you don't believe me," he cries, a little hot, "you can go and look at the copra house. It's half empty to this blessèd hour."

"I shouldn't be much the better for that, you see," says I. "For all I can tell, it might have been whole empty yesterday."

"That's so," says he, with a bit of a laugh.

"By the by," I said, "what sort of a party is that priest? Seems rather a friendly sort."

At this Case laughed right out loud. "Ah," says he, "I see what ails you now! Galuchet's been at you." *Father Galoshes* was the name he went by mostly, but Case always gave it the French quirk, which was another reason we had for thinking him above the common.

"Yes, I have seen him," I says. "I made out he didn't think much of you or Captain Randall."

"That he don't!" says Case. "It was the trouble about poor Adams. The last day, when he lay dying, there was young Buncombe round. Ever met Buncombe?"

I told him no.

"He's a cure, is Buncombe!" laughs Case. "Well, Buncombe took it in his head that as there was no other clergyman about, bar kanaka pastors, we ought to call in Father Galuchet, and have the old man administered and take the sacrament. It was all the same to me, you may suppose; but I said I thought Adams was the fellow to consult. He was jawing away about watered copra and a sight of foolery. 'Look here,' I said. 'You're pretty sick. Would you like to see Galoshes?' He sat right up on his elbow. 'Get the priest,' says he, 'get the priest, don't let me die here like a dog.' He spoke kind of fierce and eager, but sensible enough; there was nothing to say against that; so we sent and asked Galuchet if he would come. You bet he would! He jumped in his dirty linen at the thought of it. But we had reckoned without Papa. He's a hard-shell Baptist, is Papa; no papists need apply; and he took and locked the door. Buncombe told him he was bigoted, and I thought he would have had a fit. 'Bigoted!' he says. 'Me bigoted? Have I lived to hear it from a jackanapes like you?' And he made for Buncombe, and I had to hold them apart—and there was Adams in the middle, gone luny again and carrying on about copra like a born fool. It was good as the play, and I was about knocked out of time with laughing, when all of a sudden Adams sat up, clapped his hands to his chest, and went into the horrors. He died hard, did John Adams," says Case with a kind of a sudden sternness.

"And what became of the priest?" I asked.

"The priest?" says Case. "O, he was hammering on the door outside, and crying on the natives to come and beat it in, and singing out it was a soul he wished to save, and that. He was in a hell of a taking was the priest. But what would you have? Johnny had slipped his cable; no more Johnny in the market! and the administration racket clean played out. Next thing, word came to Randall the priest was praying upon Johnny's grave. Papa was pretty full, and got a club, and lit out straight for the place; and there was Galoshes on his knees, and a lot of natives looking on. You wouldn't think papa cared that much about anything, unless it was liquor; but he and the priest stuck to it two hours, slanging each other in native; and every time Galoshes tried to kneel down, papa went for him with the club. There never were such larks in Falesá. The end of it was that Captain Randall knocked over with some kind of a fit or stroke, and the priest got in his goods after all. But he was the angriest priest you ever heard of; and complained to the chiefs about the outrage, as he called it. That was no account, for our chiefs are protestant here; and anyway he had been making trouble about the drum for morning school, and they were glad to give him a wipe. Now he swears old Randall gave Adams poison or something, and when the two meet they grin at each other like baboons."

He told this story as natural as could be, and like a man that enjoyed the fun; though now I come to think of it after so long, it seems rather a sickening yarn. However Case never set up to be soft, only to be square and hearty and a man all round; and to tell the truth, he puzzled me entirely.

I went home, and asked Uma if she were a *Popey*, which I had made out to be the native word for catholics.

"*E le ai!*" says she—she always used the native when she meant "no" more than usually strong, and indeed there's more of it. "No good, popey," she added.

Then I asked her about Adams and the priest, and she told me much the same yarn in her own way. So that I was left not much farther on; but inclined upon the whole, to think the bottom of the matter was the row about the sacrament, and the poisoning only talk.

The next day was a Sunday, when there was no business to be looked for. Uma asked me in the morning if I was going to "pray"; I told her she bet not; and she stopped home herself with no more words. I thought this seemed unlike a native, and a native woman, and a woman that had new clothes to show off; however, it suited me to the ground and I made the less of it. The queer thing was that I came next door to going to church after all, a thing I'm little likely to forget. I had turned out for a stroll, and heard the hymn tune up. You know how it is; if you hear folk singing, it seems to draw you; and pretty soon I found myself alongside the church. It was a little long low place, coral built, rounded off at both ends like a whale boat, a big native roof on the top of it, windows without sashes and doorways without doors. I stuck my head into one of the windows, and the sight was so new to me—for things went quite different in the islands I was acquainted with—that I stayed and looked on. The congregation sat on the floor on mats, the women on one side, the men on the other; all rigged out to kill, the women with dresses and trade hats, the men in white jackets and shirts. The hymn was over; the pastor, a big, buck kanaka, was in the pulpit preaching for his life; and by the way he wagged his hand, and worked his voice, and made his points, and seemed to argue with the folk, I made out he was a gun at the business. Well, he looked up suddenly and caught my eye; and I give you my word he staggered in the pulpit. His eyes bulged out of his head, his hand rose and pointed at me like as if against his will, and the sermon stopped right there.

It isn't a fine thing to say for yourself, but I ran away; and if the same kind of a shock was given me, I should run away again to-morrow. To see that palavering kanaka struck all of a heap at the mere sight of me, gave me a feeling as if the bottom had dropped out of the world. I went right home, and stayed there, and said nothing. You might think I would tell Uma, but that was against my system. You might have thought I would have gone over and consulted Case; but the truth was I was ashamed to speak of such a thing, I thought everyone would blurt out laughing in my face. So I held my tongue, and thought all the more, and the more I thought, the less I liked the business.

By Monday night, I got it clearly in my head I must be tabooed. A new store to stand open two days in a village, and not a man or woman come to see the trade, was past believing.

"Uma," said I, "I think I'm tabooed."

"I think so," said she.

I thought awhile whether I should ask her more, but it's a bad idea to set natives up with any notion of consulting them, so I went to Case. It was dark, and he was sitting alone, as he did mostly, smoking on the stairs.

"Case," said I, "here's a queer thing. I'm tabooed."

"O, fudge!" says he. " 'Tain't the practise in these islands."

"That may be, or it mayn't," said I. "It's the practise where I was before; you can bet I know what it's like; and I tell it you for a fact: I'm tabooed."

"Well," said he, "what have you been doing?"

"That's what I want to find out," said I.

"O, you can't be," said he; "it ain't possible. However I'll tell you what I'll do; just to put your mind at rest, I'll go round and find out for sure. Just you waltz in and talk to papa."

"Thank you," I said, "I'd rather stay right out here on the verandah: your house is so close."

"I'll call papa out here, then," says he.

"My dear fellow," I says, "I wish you wouldn't. The fact is I don't take to Mr Randall."

Case laughed, took a lantern from the store, and set out into the village. He was gone perhaps quarter of an hour; and he looked mighty serious when he came back.

"Well," said he, clapping down the lantern on the verandah steps, "I would never have believed it. I don't know where the impudence of these kanakas 'll go next, they seem to have lost all idea of respect for whites. What we want is a man of war: a German, if we could—they know how to manage kanakas."

"I *am* tabooed then?" I cried.

"Something of the sort," said he. "It's the worst thing of the kind I've heard of yet. But I'll stand by you, Wiltshire, man to man. You come round here tomorrow about nine and we'll have it out with the chiefs. They're afraid of me; or they used to be, but their heads are so big by now I don't know what to think. Understand me, Wiltshire, I don't count this your quarrel," he went on with a great deal of resolution; "I count it all of our quarrel, I count it the White Man's Quarrel, and I'll stand to it through thick and thin, and there's my hand on it."

"Have you found out what's the reason?" I asked.

"Not yet," said Case. "But we'll fix them down tomorrow."

Altogether I was pretty well pleased with his attitude, and almost more the next day when we met to go before the chiefs, to see him so stern and resolved. The chiefs awaited us in one of their big oval houses, which was marked out to us from a long way off by the crowd about the eaves, a hundred strong if there was one, men, women and children. Many of the men were on their way to work and wore green wreaths; and it put me in thoughts of the first of May at home. This crowd opened and buzzed about the pair of us as we went in, with a sudden angry animation. Five chiefs were there, four mighty stately men, the fifth old and puckered. They sat on mats in their white kilts and jackets; they had fans in their hands like fine ladies; and two of the younger ones wore catholic medals, which gave me matter of reflection. Our place was set and the mats laid for us over against these grandees on the near side of the house; the midst was empty; the crowd, close at our backs, murmured and craned and jostled to look on, and the shadows of them tossed in front of us on the clean pebbles of the floor. I was just a hair put out by the excitement of the commons, but the quiet, civil appearance of the chiefs reassured me: all the more when their spokesman began and made a long speech in a low tone of voice, sometimes waving his hand toward Case, sometimes toward me, and sometimes knocking with his knuckles on the mat. One thing was clear: there was no sign of anger in the chiefs.

"What's he been saying?" I asked, when he had done.

"O, just that they're glad to see you, and they understand by me you wish to make some kind of a complaint, and you're to fire away, and they'll do the square thing."

"It took a precious long time to say that," said I.

"O, the rest was sawder and *bonjour* and that," says Case—"you know what kanakas are!"

"Well, they don't get much *bonjour* out of me," said I. "You tell them who I am. I'm a white man, and a British Subject, and no end of a big chief at home; and I've come here to do them good and bring them civilisation; and no sooner have I got my trade sorted out, than they go and taboo me and no one dare come near my place! Tell them I don't mean to fly in the face of anything legal; and if what they want's a present, I'll do what's fair. I don't blame any man looking out for himself, tell them, for that's human nature; but if they think they're going to come any of their native ideas over me, they'll find themselves mistaken. And tell them plain, that I demand the reason of this treatment as a White Man and a British Subject."

That was my speech. I know how to deal with kanakas; give them plain sense and fair dealing, and I'll do them that much justice, they knuckle under every time. They haven't any real government or any real law, that's what you've got to knock into their heads; and even if they had, it would be a good joke if it was to apply to a white man. It would be a strange thing if we came all this way and couldn't do what we pleased. The mere idea has always put my monkey up, and I rapped my speech out pretty big. Then Case translated it, or made believe to, rather; and the first chief replied, and then a second and a third, all in the same style, easy and genteel but solemn underneath. Once a question was put to Case, and he answered it, and all hands (both chiefs and commons) laughed out loud and looked at me. Last of all, the puckered old fellow and the big young chief that spoke first, started in to put Case through a kind of catechism. Sometimes I made out that Case was trying to fence, and they stuck to him like hounds, and the sweat ran down his face, which was no very pleasant sight to me; and at some of his answers, the crowd moaned and murmured, which was a worse hearing. It's a cruel shame I knew no native; for (as I now believe) they were asking Case about my marriage, and he must have had a tough job of it to clear his feet. But leave Case alone: he had the brains to run a parliament.

"Well, is that all?" I asked, when a pause came.

"Come along," says he, mopping his face. "I'll tell you outside."

"Do you mean they won't take the taboo off?" I cried.

"It's something queer," said he. "I'll tell you outside. Better come away."

"I won't take it at their hands," cried I. "I ain't that kind of a man. You don't find me turn my back on a parcel of kanakas."

"You'd better," said Case.

He looked at me with a signal in his eye; and the five chiefs looked at me civilly enough but kind of pointed; and the people looked at me and craned and jostled. I remembered the folks that watched my house, and how the pastor had jumped in his pulpit at the bare sight of me; and the whole business seemed so out of the way that I rose and followed Case. The crowd opened again to let us through, but wider than before, the children on the skirts running and singing out; and as we two white men walked away, they all stood and watched us.

"And now," said I, "what is all this about?"

"The truth is I can't rightly make it out myself. They have a down on you," says Case.

"Taboo a man because they have a down on him!" I cried. "I never heard the like."

"It's worse than that, you see," said Case. "You ain't tabooed, I told you that couldn't be. The people won't go near you, Wiltshire; and there's where it is."

"They won't go near me? What do you mean by that? Why won't they go near me?" I cried.

Case hesitated. "Seems they're frightened," says he, in a low voice.

I stopped dead short. "Frightened?" I repeated. "Are you gone crazy, Case? What are they frightened of?"

"I wish I could make out," Case answered, shaking his head.

"Appears like one of their tomfool superstitions. That's what I don't cotton to," he said; "it's like the business about Vigours."

"I'd like to know what you mean by that, and I'll trouble you to tell me," says I.

"Well, you know, Vigours lit out and left all standing," said he. "It was some superstition business—I never got the hang of it—but it began to look bad before the end."

"I've heard a different story about that," said I, "and I had better tell you so. I heard he ran away because of you."

"O, well, I suppose he was ashamed to tell the truth," says Case; "I guess he thought it silly. And it's a fact that I packed him off. 'What would you do, old man?' says he—'Get,' says I, 'and not think twice about it.' I was the gladdest kind of man to see him clear away. It ain't my notion to turn my back on a mate when he's in a tight place; but there was that much trouble in the village that I couldn't see where it might likely end. I was a fool to be so much about with Vigours. They cast it up to me today; didn't you hear Maea—that's the young chief, the big one—ripping out about 'Vika'? That was him they were after; they don't seem to forget it, somehow."

"This is all very well," said I, "but it don't tell me what's wrong; it don't tell me what they're afraid of—what their idea is."

"Well, I wish I knew," said Case. "I can't say fairer than that."

"You might have asked, I think," says I.

"And so I did," says he; "but you must have seen for yourself, unless you're blind, that the asking got the other way. I'll go as far as I dare for another white man; but when I find I'm in the scrape myself, I think first of my own bacon. The loss of me is I'm too good natured. And I'll take the freedom of telling you, you show a queer kind of gratitude to a man who's got into all this mess along of your affairs."

"There's a thing I'm thinking of," said I. "You were a fool to be so much about with Vigours. One comfort, you haven't been much about with me. I notice you've never been inside my house. Own up, now: you had word of this before?"

"It's a fact I haven't been," said he. "It was an oversight, and I'm sorry for it, Wiltshire. But about coming now, I'll be quite plain."

"You mean you won't?" I asked.

"Awfully sorry, old man, but that's the size of it," says Case.

"In short, you're afraid?" says I.

"In short, I'm afraid," says he.

"And I'm still to be tabooed for nothing?" I asked.

"I tell you you're not tabooed," said he. "The kanakas won't go near you, that's all. And who's to make 'em? We traders have a lot of gall, I must say; we make these poor kanakas take back their laws, and take up their taboos, and that, whenever it happens to suit us. But you don't mean to say you expect a law obliging people to deal in your store whether they want to or not? You don't mean to tell me you've got the gall for that? And if you had, it would be a queer thing to propose to me. I would just like to point out to you, Wiltshire, that I'm a trader myself."

"I don't think I would talk of gall if I was you," said I. "Here's about what it comes to, as well as I can make out. None of the people are to trade with me, and they're all to trade with you. You're to have the copra, and I'm to go to the devil and shake myself. And I don't know any native, and you're the only man here worth mention that speaks English, and you have the gall to up and hint to me my life's in danger, and all you've got to tell me is, you don't know why?"

"Well, it *is* all I have to tell you," said he. "I don't know; I wish I did."

"And so you turn your back and leave me to myself: is that the position?" says I.

"If you like to put it nasty," says he. "I don't put it so. I say merely I'm going to keep clear of you, or if I don't I'll get in danger for myself."

"Well," said I, "you're a nice kind of a white man!"

"O, I understand you're riled," said he. "I would be myself. I can make excuses."

"All right," I said, "go and make excuses somewhere else. Here's my way, there's yours."

With that we parted, and I went straight home, in a holy temper, and found Uma trying on a lot of trade goods like a baby.

"Here," I said, "you quit that foolery. Here's a pretty mess to have made—as if I wasn't bothered enough anyway! And I thought I told you to get dinner?"

And then I believe I gave her a bit of the rough side of my tongue, as she deserved. She stood up at once, like a sentry to his officer; for I must say she was always well brought up and had a great respect for whites.

"And now," says I, "you belong round here, you're bound to understand this. What am I tabooed for anyway? or if I ain't tabooed, what makes the folks afraid of me?"

She stood and looked at me with eyes like saucers.

"You no savvy?" she gasps at last.

"No," said I. "How would you expect me to? We don't have any such craziness where I come from."

"Ese no tell you?" she asked again.

(*Ese* was the name the natives had for Case; it may mean foreign, or extraordinary; or it might mean a mummy apple; but most like it was only his own name misheard and put in the kanaka spelling.)

"Not much!" said I.

"Damn Ese," she cried.

You might think it was funny to hear this kanaka girl come out with a big swear. No such thing. There was no swearing in her; no, nor anger; she was beyond anger, and meant the word simple and serious. She stood there straight as she said it; I cannot justly say that ever I saw a woman look like that before or after, and it struck me mum. Then she made a kind of an obeisance, but it was the proudest kind, and threw her hands out open.

"I 'shamed," she said. "I think you savvy. Ese he tell me you savvy, he tell me you no mind—tell me you love me too much. Taboo belong me," she said, touching herself on the bosom, as she had done upon our wedding night. "Now I go 'way, taboo he go 'way too. Then you get too much copra. You like more better, I think. Tofá, alii," says she in the native—"Farewell, chief!"

"Hold on," I cried. "Don't be in such a blamed hurry."

She looked at me sidelong with a smile. "You see, you get copra," says she, the same as you might offer candies to a child.

"Uma," said I, "hear reason. I didn't know, and that's a fact; and Case seems to have played it pretty mean upon the pair of us. But I do know now, and I don't mind: I love you too much. You no go 'way, you no leave me, I too much sorry."

"You no love me!" she cried, "you talk me bad words!" And she threw herself in a corner on the floor, and began to cry.

Well, I'm no scholar, but I wasn't born yesterday, and I thought the worst of that trouble was over. However, there she lay—her back turned, her face to the wall—and shook with sobbing like a little child, so that her feet jumped with it. It's strange how it hits a man when he's in love; for there's no use mincing things; kanaka and all, I was in love with her, or just as good. I tried to take her hand, but she would none of that. "Uma," I said, "there's no sense in carrying on like this. I want you stop here, I want my little wifie, I tell you true."

"No tell me true!" she sobbed.

"All right," says I, "I'll wait till you're through with this." And I sat right down beside her on the floor, and set to smoothe her hair with my hand. At first she wriggled away when I touched her; then she seemed to notice me no more; then her sobs grew gradually less and presently stopped; and the next thing I knew, she raised her face to mine.

"You tell me true? You like me stop?" she asked.

"Uma," I said, "I would rather have you than all the copra in the South Seas," which was a very big expression, and the strangest thing was that I meant it.

She threw her arms about me, sprang close up, and pressed her face to mine in the island way of kissing, so that I was all wetted with her tears and my heart went out to her wholly. I never had anything so near me as this little brown bit of a girl. Many things went together and all helped to turn my head. She was pretty enough to eat; it seemed she was my only friend in that queer place;

I was ashamed that I had spoken rough to her; and she was a woman, and my wife, and a kind of a baby besides that I was sorry for; and the salt of her tears was in my mouth. And I forgot Case and the natives; and I forgot that I knew nothing of the story, or only remembered it to banish the remembrance; and I forgot that I was to get no copra and so could make no livelihood; and I forgot my employers, and the strange kind of service I was doing them, when I preferred my fancy to their business; and I forgot even that Uma was no true wife of mine, but just a maid beguiled, and that in a pretty shabby style. But that is to look too far on. I will come to that part of it next.

It was late before we thought of getting dinner. The stove was out, and gone stone-cold; but we fired up after awhile, and cooked each a dish, helping and hindering each other, and making a play of it like children. I was so greedy of her nearness that I sat down to dinner with my lass upon my knee, made sure of her with one hand, and ate with the other. Ay, and more than that. She was the worst cook I suppose God made; the things she set her hand to, it would have sickened an entire horse to eat of; yet I made my meal that day on Uma's cookery, and can never call to mind to have been better pleased.

I didn't pretend to myself, and I didn't pretend to her. I saw I was clean gone; and if she was to make a fool of me, she must. And I suppose it was this that set her talking, for now she made sure that we were friends. A lot she told me, sitting in my lap and eating my dish, as I ate hers, from foolery: a lot about herself and her mother and Case, all which would be very tedious and fill sheets if I set it down in Beach de Mar, but which I must give a hint of in plain English—and one thing about myself, which had a very big effect on my concerns, as you are soon to hear.

It seems she was born in one of the Line islands; had been only two or three years in these parts, where she had come with a white man who was married to her mother and then died; and only the one year in Falesá. Before that, they had been a good deal on the move, trekking about after the white man, who was one of these rolling stones that keep going round after a soft job. They talk about looking for gold at the end of a rainbow; but if a man wants an employment that'll last him till he dies, let him start out on the soft-job hunt. There's meat and drink in it too, and beer and skittles; for you never hear of them starving and rarely see them sober; and as for steady sport, cockfighting isn't in the same county with it. Anyway, this beachcomber carried the woman and her daughter all over the shop, but mostly to out of the way islands, where there were no police and he thought perhaps the soft-job hung out. I've my own view of this old party; but I was just as glad he had kept Uma clear of Apia and Papeete and these flash towns. At last he struck Fale-alii on this island, got some trade the Lord knows how! muddled it all away in the usual style, and died worth next to nothing, bar a bit of land at Falesá that he had got for a bad debt, which was what put it in the minds of the mother and daughter to come there and live. It seems Case encouraged them all he could, and helped to get their house built. He was very kind those days, and gave Uma trade, and there is no doubt he had his eye on her from the beginning. However, they had scarce settled, when up turned a young man, a native, and wanted to marry her. He was a small chief, and had some fine mats and old songs in his family, and was "very pretty," Uma said; and altogether it was an extraordinary match for a penniless girl and an out-islander.

At the first word of this, I got downright sick with jealousy.

"And you mean to say you would have married him!" I cried.

"*Ioe*," says she. "I like too much!"

"Well!" I said. "And suppose I had come round after?"

"I like you more better now," said she. "But suppose I marry Ioane, I one good wife. I no common kanaka: good girl!" says she.

Well, I had to be pleased with that; but I promise you I didn't care about the business one little bit, and liked the end of that yarn better than the beginning. For it seems this proposal of marriage was the start of all the trouble. It seems, before that, Uma and her mother had been looked down upon of course for kinless folk and out-islanders, but nothing to hurt; and even when Ioane came forward there was less trouble at first than might have been looked for. And then all of a sudden, about six months before my coming, Ioane backed out and left that part of the island, and from that day to this, Uma and her mother had found themselves alone. None called at their house, none spoke to them on the roads. If they went to church, the other women drew their mats away and left them in a clear place by themselves. It was a regular excommunication, like what you read of in the middle ages; and the cause or sense of it beyond guessing. It was some *tala pepelo*, Uma said, some lie, some calumny; and all she knew of it was that the girls who had been jealous of her luck with Ioane used to twit her with his desertion, and cry out, when they met her alone in the woods, that she would never be married. "They tell me no man he marry me. He too much 'fraid," she said.

The only soul that came about them after this desertion was Master Case; even he was chary of showing himself, and turned up mostly by night; and pretty soon he began to table his cards and make up to Uma. I was still sore about Ioane, and when Case turned up in the same line of business, I cut up downright rough.

"Well," I said sneering, "and I suppose you thought Case 'very pretty' and 'liked too much.'"

"Now you talk silly," said she. "White man he come here, I marry him all-e-same kanaka; very well then, he marry me all-e-same white woman. Suppose he no marry, he go 'way, woman he stop. All-e-same thief; empty hand, Tonga-heart—no can love! Now you come marry me; you big heart—you no 'shamed island girl. That thing I love you for too much. I proud."

I don't know that ever I felt sicker all the days of my life. I laid down my fork and I put away 'the island girl'; I didn't seem somehow to have any use for either; and I went and walked up and down in the house, and Uma followed me with her eyes, for she was troubled, and small wonder! But troubled was no word for it with me; I so wanted, and so feared, to make a clean breast of the sweep that I had been.

And just then there came a sound of singing out of the sea; it sprang up suddenly clear and near, as the boat turned the headland; and Uma, running to the window, cried out it was "Misi" come upon his rounds.

I thought it was a strange thing I should be glad to have a missionary; but if it was strange, it was still true.

"Uma," said I, "you stop here in this room, and don't budge a foot out of it till I come back."

Chapter III

 # The Missionary

As I came out on the verandah, the mission boat was shooting for the mouth of the river. She was a long whale boat painted white; a bit of an awning astern; a native pastor crouched on the wedge of poop, steering; some four and twenty paddles flashing and dipping, true to the boat-song; and the missionary under the awning, in his white clothes, reading in a book, and set him up! It was pretty to see and hear; there's no smarter sight in the islands than a missionary boat with a good crew and a good pipe to them; and I considered it for half a minute with a bit of envy perhaps, and then strolled towards the river.

From the opposite side there was another man aiming for the same place, but he ran and got there first. It was Case; doubtless his idea was to keep me apart from the missionary who might serve me as interpreter; but my mind was upon other things, I was thinking how he had jockeyed us about the marriage, and tried his hand on Uma before; and at the sight of him, rage flew in my nostrils.

"Get out of that, you low, swindling thief!" I cried.

"What's that you say?" says he.

I gave him the word again, and rammed it down with a good oath. "And if ever I catch you within six fathoms of my house," I cried, "I'll clap a bullet in your measly carcase."

"You must do as you like about your house," said he, "where I told you I have no thought of going. But this is a public place."

"It's a place where I have private business," said I. "I have no idea of a hound like you eavesdropping, and I give you notice to clear out."

"I don't take it though," says Case.

"I'll show you, then," said I.

"We'll have to see about that," said he.

He was quick with his hands, but he had neither the height nor the weight, being a flimsy creature alongside a man like me; and besides I was blazing to that height of wrath that I could have bit into a chisel. I gave him first the one and then the other, so that I could hear his head rattle and crack, and he went down straight.

"Have you had enough?" cries I. But he only looked up white and blank, and the blood spread upon his face like wine upon a napkin. "Have you had enough?" I cried again. "Speak up, and don't lie malingering there, or I'll take my feet to you!"

He sat up at that, and held his head—by the look of him you could see it was spinning—and the blood poured on his pyjamas.

"I've had enough for this time," says he, and he got up staggering and went off by the way that he had come.

The boat was close in; I saw the missionary had laid his book to one side, and I smiled to myself. "He'll know I'm a man, anyway," thinks I.

This was the first time, in all my years in the Pacific, I had ever exchanged two words with any missionary; let alone asked one for a favour. I didn't like the lot, no trader does; they look down upon us and make no concealment; and besides they're partly kanaka-ised, and suck up with natives instead of with other white men like themselves. I had on a rig of clean, striped pyjamas, for of course I had dressed decent to go before the chiefs; but when I saw the missionary step out of his boat in the regular uniform, white duck clothes, pith helmet, white shirt and tie, and yellow boots to his feet, I could have bunged stones at him. As he came nearer, queering me pretty curious (because of the fight I suppose) I saw he looked mortal sick, for the truth was he had a fever on and had just had a chill in the boat.

"Mr Tarleton, I believe?" says I, for I had got his name.

"And you, I suppose, are the new trader?" says he.

"I want to tell you first that I don't hold with missions," I went on, "and that I think you and the likes of you do a sight of harm, filling up the natives with old wives' tales and bumptiousness."

"You are perfectly entitled to your opinions," says he, looking a bit ugly, "but I have no call to hear them."

"It so happens that you've got to hear them," I said. "I'm no missionary nor missionary lover; I'm no kanaka nor favourer of kanakas: I'm just a trader, I'm just a common, low, god-damned white man and British subject, the sort you would like to wipe your boots on. I hope that's plain."

"Yes, my man," said he. "It's more plain than creditable. When you are sober, you'll be sorry for this."

He tried to pass on, but I stopped him with my hand. The kanakas were beginning to growl; guess they didn't like my tone, for I spoke to that man as free as I would to you.

"Now you can't say I've deceived you," said I, "and I can go on. I want a service, I want two services in fact; and if you care to give me them, I'll perhaps take more stock in what you call your christianity."

He was silent for a moment. Then he smiled. "You are rather a strange sort of man," says he.

"I'm the sort of a man God made me," says I. "I don't set up to be a gentleman," I said.

"I am not quite so sure," said he. "And what can I do for you, Mr ———?"

"Wiltshire," I says, "though I'm mostly called Welsher; but Wiltshire is the way it's spellt, if the people on the beach could only get their tongues about it. And what do I want? Well, I'll tell you the first thing. I'm what you call a sinner—what I call a sweep—and I want you to help me make it up to a person I've deceived."

He turned and spoke to his crew in the native. "And now I am at your service," said he, "but only for the time my crew are dining. I must be much farther down the coast before night. I was delayed at Papa-mālūlū till this morning, and I have an engagement in Fale-alii tomorrow night."

I led the way to my house in silence and rather pleased with myself for the way I had managed the talk, for I like a man to keep his self-respect.

"I was sorry to see you fighting," says he.

"O, that's part of a yarn I want to tell you," I said. "That's service number two. After you've heard it, you'll let me know whether you're sorry or not."

We walked right in through the store, and I was surprised to find Uma had cleared away the dinner things. This was so unlike her ways, that I saw she had done it out of gratitude, and liked her the better. She and Mr Tarleton called each other by name, and he was very civil to her seemingly. But I thought little of that; they can always find civility for a kanaka; it's us white men they lord it over. Besides I didn't want much Tarleton just then: I was going to do my pitch.

"Uma," said I, "give us your marriage certificate." She looked put out. "Come," said I. "You can trust me. Hand it up."

She had it about her person as usual; I believe she thought it was a pass to heaven, and if she died without having it handy she would go to hell. I couldn't see where she put it the first time, I couldn't see now where she took it from; it seemed to jump in her hand like that Blavatsky business in the papers. But it's the same way with all island women, and I guess they're taught it when young.

"Now," said I, with the certificate in my hand, "I was married to this girl by Black Jack the negro. The certificate was wrote by Case, and it's a dandy piece of literature, I promise you. Since then I've found that there's a kind of cry in the place against this wife of mine, and so long as I keep her, I cannot trade. Now what would any man do in my place, if he was a man?" I said. "The first thing he would do is this, I guess." And I took and tore up the certificate and bunged the pieces on the floor.

"Aué!" cried Uma, and began to clap her hands, but I caught one of them in mine.

"And the second thing that he would do," said I, "if he was what I would call a man, and you would call a man, Mr Tarleton, is to bring the girl right before you or any other missionary, and to up and say: 'I was wrong married to this wife of mine, but I think a heap of her, and now I want to be married to her right.' Fire away, Mr Tarleton. And I guess you'd better do it in native; it'll please the old lady," I said, giving her the proper name of a man's wife upon the spot.

So we had in two of the crew to witness, and were spliced in our own house; and the parson prayed a good bit, I must say, but not so long as some, and shook hands with the pair of us.

"Mr Wiltshire," he says, when he had made out the lines and packed off the witnesses, "I have to thank you for a very lively pleasure. I have rarely performed the marriage ceremony with more grateful emotions."

That was what you would call talking. He was going on besides with more of it, and I was ready for as much taffy as he had in stock, for I felt good. But Uma had been taken up with something half through the marriage, and cut straight in.

"How your hand he get hurt?" she asked.

"You ask Case's head, old lady," says I.

She jumped with joy, and sang out.

"You haven't made much of a christian of this one," says I to Mr Tarleton.

"We didn't think her one of our worst," says he, "when she was at Fale-alii; and if Uma bears malice, I shall be tempted to fancy she has good cause."

"Well, there we are at service number two," said I. "I want to tell you our yarn, and see if you can let a little daylight in."

"Is it long?" he asked.

"Yes," I said, "it's a goodish bit of a yarn."

"Well, I'll give you all the time I can spare," says he, looking at his watch. "But I must tell you fairly I haven't eaten since five this morning; and unless you can let me have something, I am not likely to eat again before seven or eight tonight."

"By God, we'll give you dinner!" I cried.

I was a little caught up at my swearing, just when all was going straight; and so was the missionary I suppose, but he made believe to look out of the window and thanked us.

So we ran him up a bit of a meal. I was bound to let the old lady have a hand in it, to show off; so I deputised her to brew the tea. I don't think I ever met such tea as she turned out. But that was not the worst, for she got round with the salt-box, which she considered an extra European touch, and turned my stew into sea water. Altogether, Mr Tarleton had a devil of a dinner of it; but he had plenty entertainment by the way, for all the while that we were cooking, and afterwards when he was making believe to eat, I kept posting him up on Master Case and the beach of Falesá, and he putting questions that showed he was following close.

"Well," said he at last, "I am afraid you have a dangerous enemy. This man Case is very clever and seems really wicked. I must tell you I have had my eye on him for nearly a year, and have rather had the worst of our encounters. About the time when the last representative of your firm ran so suddenly away, I had a letter from Namu, the native pastor, begging me to come to Falesá at my earliest convenience, as his flock were all 'adopting catholic practices.' I had great confidence in Namu; I fear it only shows how easily we are deceived. No one could hear him preach and not be persuaded he was a man of extraordinary parts. All our islanders easily acquire a kind of eloquence, and can roll out and illustrate with a great deal of vigour and fancy secondhand sermons; but Namu's sermons are his own, and I cannot deny that I have found them means of grace. Moreover he has a keen curiosity in secular things, does not fear work, is clever at carpentering, and has made himself so much respected among the neighbouring pastors that we call him, in a jest which is half serious, the Bishop of the East. In short I was proud of the man; all the more puzzled by his letter; and took occasion to come this way. The morning before my arrival, Vigours had been set on board the *Lion*, and Namu was perfectly at his ease, apparently ashamed of his letter, and quite unwilling to explain it. This of course I could not allow; and he ended by confessing that he had been much concerned to find his people using the sign of the cross, but since he had learned the explanation his mind was satisfied. For Vigours had the Evil Eye, a common thing in a country of Europe called Italy, where men were

often struck dead by that kind of devil; and it appeared the sign of the cross was a charm against its power.

" 'And I explain it, Misi,' said Namu in this way. 'The country in Europe is a Popey country, and the devil of the Evil Eye may be a catholic devil, or at least used to catholic ways. So then I reasoned thus; if this sign of the cross were used in a Popey manner, it would be sinful; but when it is used only to protect men from a devil, which is a thing harmless in itself, the sign too must be harmless. For the sign is neither good nor bad, even as a bottle is neither good nor bad. But if the bottle be full of gin, the gin is bad; and if the sign be made in idolatry, so is the idolatry bad.' And very like a native pastor, he had a text apposite about the casting out of devils.

" 'And who has been telling you about the Evil Eye?' I asked.

"He admitted it was Case. Now I am afraid you will think me very narrow, Mr Wiltshire, but I must tell you I was displeased, and cannot think a trader at all a good man to advise or have an influence upon my pastors. And besides there had been some flying talk in the country of old Adams and his being poisoned, to which I had paid no great heed; but it came back to me at the moment.

" 'And is this Case a man of sanctified life?' I asked.

"He admitted he was not; for though he did not drink, he was profligate with women and had no religion.

" 'Then,' said I, 'I think the less you have to do with him the better.'

"But it is not easy to have the last word with a man like Namu; he was ready in a moment with an illustration. 'Misi,' said he, 'you have told me there were wise men, not pastors, not even holy, who knew many things useful to be taught, about trees for instance, and beasts, and to print books, and about the stones that are burned to make knives of. Such men teach you in your college, and you learn from them, but take care not to learn to be unholy. Misi, Case is my college.'

"I knew not what to say. Mr Vigours had evidently been driven out of Falesá by the machinations of Case and with something not very unlike the collusion of my pastor. I called to mind it was Namu who had reassured me about Adams and traced the rumour to the ill will of the priest. And I saw I must inform myself more thoroughly from an impartial source. There is an old rascal of a chief here, Faiaso, whom I daresay you saw today at the council; he has been all his life turbulent and sly, a great fomenter of rebellions, and a thorn in the side of the mission and the island. For all that he is very shrewd, and except in politics or about his own misdemeanours, a teller of the truth. I went to his house, told him what I had heard, and besought him to be frank. I do not think I had ever a more painful interview. Perhaps you will understand me, Mr Wiltshire, if I tell you that I am perfectly serious in these old-wives' tales with which you reproached me, and as anxious to do well for these islands as you can be to please and to protect your pretty wife. And you are to remember that I thought Namu a paragon, and was proud of the man as one of the first ripe fruits of the mission. And now I was informed that he had fallen in a sort of dependence upon Case. The beginning of it was not corrupt; it began doubtless in fear and respect produced by trickery and pretence; but I was shocked to find that another element had been lately added, that Namu helped himself in the store, and was believed to be deep in Case's debt. Whatever the trader said, that Namu believed with trembling. He was not alone in this; many in the village lived in a similar subjection; but Namu's case was the most influential, it was through Namu Case had wrought most evil; and with a certain following among the chiefs, and the pastor in his pocket, the man was as good as master of the village. You know something of Vigours and Adams; but perhaps you have never heard of old Underhill, Adams's predecessor. He was a quiet, mild old fellow, I remember, and we were told he had died suddenly: white men die very suddenly in Falesá. The truth, as I now heard it, made my blood run cold. It seems he was struck with a general palsy, all of him dead but one eye, which he continually winked. Word was started that the helpless old man was now a devil; and this vile fellow Case worked upon the natives' fears, which he professed to share, and pretended he durst not go into the house alone. At last a grave was dug, and the living body buried at the far end of the village. Namu, my pastor, whom I had helped to educate, offered up prayer at the hateful scene.

"I felt myself in a very difficult position. Perhaps too it was my duty to have denounced Namu and had him deposed; perhaps I think so now; but at the time, it seemed less clear. He had a great influence, it might prove greater than mine. The natives are prone to superstition; perhaps by stirring them up, I might but ingrain and spread these dangerous fancies. And Namu besides, apart from this novel and accursed influence, was a good pastor, an able man and spiritually minded. Where should I look for a better? how was I to find as good? At that moment with Namu's failure fresh in my view, the work of my life appeared a mockery; hope was dead in me; I would rather repair such tools as I had, than go abroad in quest of others that must certainly prove worse; and a scandal is, at the best, a thing to be avoided when humanly possible. Right or wrong then, I determined on a quiet course. All that night I denounced and reasoned with the erring pastor; twitted him with his ignorance and want of faith; twitted him with his wretched attitude, making clean the outside of the cup and platter, callously helping at a murder, childishly flying in excitement about a few childish, unnecessary and inconvenient gestures; and long before day, I had him on his knees and bathed in tears of what seemed a genuine repentance. On Sunday I took the pulpit in the morning and preached from First Kings, nineteenth, on the fire, the earth-quake and the voice: distinguishing the true spiritual power, and referring with such plainness as I dared to recent events in Falesá. The effect produced was great; and it was much increased, when Namu rose in his turn, and confessed that he had been wanting in faith and conduct, and was convinced of sin. So far, then, all was well; but there was one unfortunate circumstance. It was nearing the time of our 'May' in the island, when the native contributions to the mission are received; it fell in my duty to make a notification on the subject; and this gave my enemy his chance, by which he was not slow to profit.

"News of the whole proceedings must have been carried to Case as soon as church was over; and the same afternoon he made an occasion to meet me in the midst of the village. He came up with so much intentness and animosity that I felt it would be damaging to avoid him.

" 'So,' says he in native, 'here is the holy man. He has been preaching against me, but that was not in his heart. He has been preaching upon the love of God, but that was not in his heart—it was between his teeth. Will you know what was in his heart?' cries he. 'I will show it you.' And making a snatch at my head, he made believe to pluck out a dollar, and held it in the air.

"There went that rumour through the crowd with which Polynesians receive a prodigy. As for myself, I stood amazed. The thing was a common, conjuring trick, which I have seen performed at home a score of times; but how was I to convince the villagers of that? I wished I had learned legerdemain instead of Hebrew, that I might have paid the fellow out with his own coin. But there I was, I could not stand there silent, and the best that I could find to say was weak.

" 'I will trouble you not to lay hands on me again,' said I.

" 'I have no such thought,' said he, 'nor will I deprive you of your dollar. Here it is,' he said, and flung it at my feet. I am told it lay where it fell three days."

"I must say it was well played," said I.

"O, he is clever," said Mr Tarleton, "and you can now see for yourself how dangerous. He was a party to the horrid death of the paralytic; he is accused of poisoning Adams; he drove Vigours out of the place by lies that might have led to murder; and there is no question but he has now made up his mind to rid himself of you. How he means to try, we have no guess; only be sure it's something new. There is no end to his readiness and invention."

"He gives himself a sight of trouble," says I. "And after all, what for?"

"Why, how many tons of copra may they make in this district?" asked the missionary.

"I daresay as much as sixty tons," says I.

"And what is the profit to the local trader?" he asked.

"You may call it three pounds," said I.

"Then you can reckon for yourself how much he does it for," said Mr Tarleton. "But the more important thing is to defeat him. It is clear he spread some report against Uma, in order to isolate and have his wicked will of her; failing of that, and seeing a new rival come upon the scene, he used her in a different way. Now the first point to find out is about Namu. Uma, when people began to leave you and your mother alone, what did Namu do?"

"Stop away all-e-same," says Uma.

"I fear the dog has returned to his vomit," said Mr Tarleton. "And now what am I to do for you? I will speak to Namu, I will warn him he is observed; it will be strange if he allow anything to go on amiss, when he is put upon his guard. At the same time, this precaution may fail, and then you must turn elsewhere. You have two people at hand to whom you might apply. There is first of all the priest, who might protect you by the catholic interest; they are a wretchedly small body, but they count two chiefs. And then there is old Faiaso. Ah, if it had been some years ago, you would have needed no one else; but his influence is much reduced, it has gone into Maea's hands, and Maea, I fear, is one of Case's jackalls. In fine, if the worst comes to the worst, you must send up or come yourself to Fale-alii, and though I am not due at this end of the island for a month, I will see what can be done."

So Mr Tarleton said farewell; and half an hour later, the crew were singing and the paddles flashing in the missionary boat.

Chapter IV

Devil-Work

Near a month went by without much doing. The same night of our marriage, Galoshes called round, made himself mighty civil, and got into a habit of dropping in about dark and smoking his pipe with the family. He could talk to Uma of course, and started to teach me native and French at the same time. He was a kind old buffer, though the dirtiest you would wish to see, and he muddled me up with foreign languages worse than the tower of Babel.

That was one employment we had, and it made me feel less lonesome; but there was no profit in the thing; for though the priest came and sat and yarned, none of his folks could be enticed into my store; and if it hadn't been for the other occupation I struck out, there wouldn't have been a pound of copra in the house. This was the idea: Fa'avao (Uma's mother) had a score of bearing trees. Of course, we could get no labour, being all as good as tabooed. And the two women and I turned to and made copra with our own hands. It was copra to make your mouth water, when it was done—I never understood how much the natives cheated me till I had made that four hundred pounds of my own hand—and it weighed so light, I felt inclined to take and water it myself.

When we were at the job, a good many kanakas used to put in the best of the day looking on, and once that nigger turned up. He stood back with the natives, and laughed, and did the big don and the funny dog, till I began to get riled.

"Here, you, nigger!" says I.

"I don't address myself to you, sah," says the nigger. "Only speak to gen'le'um."

"I know," says I, "but it happens I was addressing myself to you, Mr Black Jack. And all I want to know is just this: did you see Case's figurehead about a week ago?"

"No, sah," says he.

"That's all right, then," says I; "for I'll show you the own brother to it, only black, in the inside of about two minutes."

And I began to walk towards him, quite slow and my hands down; only there was trouble in my eye, if anybody took the pains to look.

"You're a low, obstropulous fellow, sah," says he.

"You bet!" says I.

By that time he thought I was about as near as was convenient, and lit out so it would have done your heart good to see him travel. And that was all I saw of that precious gang, until what I am about to tell you.

It was one of my chief employments these days to go pot-hunting in the woods, which I found (as Case had told me) very rich in game. I have spoken of the cape, which shut up the village and my station from the east. A path went about the end of it, and led into the next bay. A strong wind blew here daily, and as the line of the barrier reef stopped at the end of the cape, a heavy surf ran on the shores of the bay. A little cliffy hill cut the valley in two parts, and stood close on the beach; and at high water the sea broke right on the face of it, so that all passage was stopped. Woody mountains hemmed the place all round; the barrier to the east was particularly steep and leafy; the lower parts of it, along the sea, falling in sheer black cliffs streaked with cinnabar; the upper part lumpy with the tops of the great trees. Some of the trees were bright green, and some red, and the sand of the beach as black as your shoes. Many birds hovered round the bay, some of them snow white; and the flying-fox (or vampire) flew there in broad daylight, gnashing its teeth.

For a long while I came as far as this shooting and went no farther. There was no sign of any path beyond; and the cocoapalms in the front of the foot of the valley were the last this way. For the whole "eye" of the island, as natives call the windward end, lay desert. From Falesá round about to Papa-mālūlū, there was neither house, nor man, nor planted fruit tree; and the reef being mostly absent and the shores bluff, the sea beat direct among crags, and there was scarce a landing place.

I should tell you that after I began to go in the woods, although no one offered to come near my store, I found people willing enough to pass the time of day with me where nobody could see them. And as I had begun to pick up native, and most of them had a word or two of English, I began to hold little odds and ends of conversation, not to much purpose, to be sure, but they took off the worst of the feeling. For it's a miserable thing to be made a leper of.

It chanced one day, towards the end of the month, that I was sitting in this bay in the edge of the bush, looking east, with a kanaka. I had given him a fill of tobacco, and we were making out to talk as best we could; indeed he had more English than most.

I asked him if there was no road going eastward.

"One time one road," said he. "Now he dead."

"Nobody he go there?" I asked.

"No good," said he. "Too much devil he stop there."

"Oho!" says I, "got-um plenty devil, that bush?"

"Man devil, woman devil: too much devil," said my friend. "Stop there all-e-time. Man he go there, no come back."

I thought, if this fellow was so well posted on devils and spoke of them so free, which is not common, I had better fish for a little information about myself and Uma.

"You think me one devil?" I asked.

"No think devil," said he soothingly. "Think all-e-same fool."

"Uma, she devil?" I asked again.

"No, no; no devil; devil stop bush," said the young man.

I was looking in front of me across the bay, and I saw the hanging front of the woods pushed suddenly open, and Case with a gun in his hand step forth into the sunshine on the black beach. He was got up in light pyjamas, near white, his gun sparkled, he looked mighty conspicuous; and the land crabs scuttled from all round him to their holes.

"Hullo, my friend," says I, "you no talk all-e-same true. Ese he go, he come back."

"Ese no all-e-same; Ese *Tiapolo*," says my friend; and with a good bye, slunk off among the trees.

I watched Case all round the beach, where the tide was low; and let him pass me on the homeward way to Falesá. He was in deep thought; and the birds seemed to know it, trotting quite near him on the sand or wheeling and calling in his ears. Where he passed nearest me, I could see by the working of his lips that he was talking in to himself, and what pleased me mightily, he had still my trademark on his brow. I tell you the plain truth, I had a mind to give him a gunfull in his ugly mug, but I thought better of it.

All this time, and all the time I was following home, I kept repeating that native word, which I remembered by "Polly, put the kettle on and make us all some tea": tea-a-pollo.

"Uma," says I, when I got back, "what does Tiapolo mean?"

"Devil," says she.

"I thought *aitu* was the word for that?" I said.

"*Aitu* 'nother kind of devil," said she; "stop bush, eat kanaka. Tiapolo big-chief devil, stop home; all-e-same Christian devil."

"Well then," said I. "I'm no farther forward. How can Case be Tiapolo?"

"No all-e-same," said she. "Ese belong Tiapolo; Tiapolo too much like; Ese all-e-same his son. Suppose Ese he wish something, Tiapolo he make him."

"That's mighty convenient for Ese," says I. "And what kind of things does he make for him?"

Well, out came a rigmarole of all sorts of stories, many of which (like the dollar he took from Mr Tarleton's head) were plain enough to me, but others I could make nothing of; and the thing that most surprised the kanakas was what surprised me least: namely, that he could go in the desert among all the *aitus*. Some of the boldest, however, had accompanied him, and had heard him speak with the dead and give them orders, and safe in his protection, had returned unscathed. Some said he had a church there where he worshipped Tiapolo, and Tiapolo appeared to him; others swore there was no sorcery at all, that he performed his miracles by the power of prayer, and the church was no church but a prison in which he had confined a dangerous *aitu*. Namu had been in the bush with him once, and returned glorifying God for these wonders. Altogether I began to have a glimmer of the man's position, and the means by which he had acquired it, and though I saw he was a tough nut to crack, I was noways cast down.

"Very well," said I, "I'll have a look at Master Case's place of worship myself, and we'll see about the glorifying."

At this time Uma fell in a terrible taking; if I went in the high bush, I should never return; none could go there but by the protection of Tiapolo.

"I'll chance it on God's," said I. "I'm a good sort of a fellow, Uma, as fellows go; and I guess God'll con me through."

She was silent for awhile. "I think," said she, mighty solemn; and then presently: "Victoreea he big chief?"

"You bet," said I.

"He like you too much?" she asked again.

I told her with a grin I believed the old lady was rather partial to me.

"All right," said she. "Victoreea he big chief, like you too much; no can help you here in Falesá; no can do, too far off. Maea he small chief; stop here; suppose he like you, make you all right. All-e-same God and Tiapolo. God he big chief, got too much work. Tiapolo he small chief, he like too much make-see, work very hard."

"I'll have to hand you over to Mr Tarleton," said I. "Your theology's out of its bearings, Uma."

However we stuck at this business all the evening, and with the stories she told me of the desert and its dangers, she came near frightening herself into a fit. I don't remember half a quarter of them of course, for I paid little heed; but two come back to me kind of clear.

About six miles up the coast there is a sheltered cove, they call

Fanga-anaana, "the haven full of caves." I've seen it from the sea myself, as near as I could get my boys to venture in; and it's a little strip of yellow sand. Black cliffs overhang it full of the black mouths of caves, great trees overhang the cliffs and dangle down lianas, and in one place, about the middle, a big brook pours over in a cascade. Well, there was a boat going by here with six young men of Falesá, "all very pretty," Uma said, which was the loss of them. It blew strong, there was a heavy head sea; and by the time they opened Fanga-anaana, and saw the white cascade and the shady beach, they were all tired and thirsty, and their water had run out. One proposed to land and get a drink; and being reckless fellows, they were all of the same mind except the youngest. Lotu was his name; he was a very good young gentleman and very wise; and he held out they were crazy, telling them the place was given over to spirits and devils and the dead, and there were no living folk nearer than six miles the one way and maybe twelve the other. But they laughed at his words; and being five to one, pulled in, beached the boat, and landed. It was a wonderful pleasant place, Lotu said, and the water excellent. They walked round the beach, but could see nowhere any way to mount the cliffs, which made them easier in their mind; and at last they sat down to make a meal on the food they had brought with them. They were scarce set, when there came out of the mouth of one of the black caves six of the most beautiful ladies ever seen; they had flowers in their hair, and the most beautiful breasts, and necklaces of scarlet seeds; and began to jest with these young gentlemen, and the young gentlemen to jest back with them, all but Lotu. As for Lotu, he saw there could be no living women in such a place, and ran, and flung himself in the bottom of the boat, and covered his face, and prayed. All the time the business lasted, Lotu made one clean break of prayer; and that was all he knew of it, until his friends came back, and made him sit up, and they put to sea again out of the bay, which was now quite desert, and no word of the six ladies. But what frightened Lotu worst, not one of the five remembered anything of what had passed, but they were all like drunken men, and sang and laughed in the boat, and skylarked. The wind freshened and came squally, the sea rose extraordinary high; it was such weather as any man in the islands would have turned his back to and fled home to Falesá; but these five were like crazy folk, and cracked on all sail, and drove their boat into the seas. Lotu went to the bailing; none of the others thought to help him, but sang and skylarked and carried on, and spoke singular things beyond a man's comprehension, and laughed out loud when they said them. So the rest of that day, Lotu bailed for his life in the bottom of the boat, and was all drenched with sweat and cold sea water; and none heeded him. Against all expectation, they came safe in a dreadful tempest to Papa-mālūlū, where the palms were singing out and the cocoanuts flying like cannon balls about the village green; and the same night the five young gentlemen sickened and spoke never a reasonable word until they died.

"And do you mean to tell me you can swallow a yarn like that?" I asked.

She told me the thing was well known, and with handsome young men alone, it was even common. But this was the only case where five had been slain the same day and in a company by the love of the women devils; and it had made a great stir in the island; and she would be crazy if she doubted.

"Well anyway," says I, "you needn't be frightened about me. I've got no use for the women devils; you're all the women I want, and all the devil too, old lady."

To that she answered there were other sorts, and she had seen one with her own eyes. She had gone one day alone to the next bay, and perhaps got too near the margin of the bad place. The boughs of the high bush overshadowed her from the kant of the hill; but she herself was outside in a flat place, very stony and grow-ing full of young mummy-apples, four and five feet high. It was a dark day in the rainy season; and now there came squalls that tore off the leaves and sent them flying, and now it was all still as in a house. It was in one of these still times, that a whole gang of birds and flying-foxes came pegging out of the bush like creatures fright-ened. Presently after she heard a rustle nearer hand, and saw com-ing out of the margin of the trees among the mummy-apples, the appearance of a lean, gray, old boar. It seemed to think as it came, like a person; and all of a sudden, as she looked at it coming, she was aware it was no boar but a thing that was a man with a man's thoughts. At that she ran, and the pig after her, and as the pig ran it hollered aloud, so that the place rang with it.

"I wish I had been there with my gun," said I. "I guess the pig would have hollered so as to surprise himself."

But she told me a gun was of no use with the like of these, which were the spirits of the dead.

Well, this kind of talk put in the evening, which was the best of it; but of course it didn't change my notion; and the next day, with my gun and a good knife, I set off upon a voyage of discovery. I made as near as I could for the place where I had seen Case come out; for if it was true he had some kind of establishment in the bush, I reckoned I should find a path. The beginning of the desert was marked off by a wall—to call it so, for it was more of a long mound of stones; they say it reaches right across the island, but how they know it is another question, for I doubt if anyone has made the journey in a hundred years; the natives sticking chiefly to the sea and their little colonies along the coast, and that part being mortal high and steep and full of cliffs. Up to the west side of the wall, the ground has been cleared, and there are cocoa-palms, and mummy-apples, and guavas, and lots of sensitive. Just across, the bush begins outright; high bush at that: trees going up like the masts of ships, and ropes of liana hanging down like a ship's rigging, and nasty orchids growing in the forks like funguses. The ground, where there was no underwood, looked to be a heap of boulders. I saw many green pigeons which I might have shot, only I was there with a different idea; a number of butterflies flopped up and down along the ground like dead leaves; sometimes I would hear a bird calling, sometimes the wind overhead, and always the sea along the coast.

But the queerness of the place, it's more difficult to tell of; unless to one who has been alone in the high bush himself. The brightest kind of a day, it is always dim down there. A man can see to the end of nothing; whichever way he looks, the wood shuts up, one bough folding with another, like the fingers of your hand; and whenever he listens, he hears always something new—men talking, children laughing, the strokes of an axe a far way ahead of him, and sometimes a sort of quick, stealthy scurry near at hand that makes him jump and look to his weapons. It's all very well for him to tell himself that he's alone, bar trees and birds; he can't make out to believe it: whichever way he turns, the whole place seems to be alive and looking on. Don't think it was Uma's yarns that put me out; I don't value native talk a fourpenny piece: it's a thing that's natural in the bush, and that's the end of it.

As I got near the top of the hill, for the ground of the wood goes up in this place steep as a ladder, the wind began to sound straight on, and the leaves to toss and switch open and let in the sun. This suited me better; it was the same noise all the time and nothing to startle. Well, I had got to a place where there was an underwood of what they call wild cocoanut—mighty pretty with its scarlet fruits—when there came a sound of singing in the wind that I thought I had never heard the like of. It was all very fine to tell myself it was the branches; I knew better. It was all very fine to tell myself it was a bird; I knew never a bird that sang like that. It rose, and swelled, and died away, and swelled again; and now I thought it was like some one weeping, only prettier; and now I thought it was like harps; and there was one thing I made sure of, it was a sight too sweet to be wholesome in a place like that. You may laugh if you like; but I declare I called to mind the six young ladies that came, with their scarlet necklaces, out of the cave at Fanga-anaana, and wondered if they sang like that. We laugh at the natives and their superstitions; but see how many traders take them up, splendidly educated white men, that have been bookkeepers (some of them) and clerks in the old country! It's my belief a superstition grows up in a place like the different kinds of weeds; and as I stood there, and listened to that wailing, I twittered in my shoes.

You may call me a coward to be frightened; I thought myself brave enough to go on ahead. But I went mighty carefully, with my gun cocked, spying all about me like a hunter, fully expecting to see a handsome young woman sitting somewhere in the bush, and fully determined (if I did) to try her with a charge of duckshot. And sure enough I had not gone far, when I met with a queer thing. The wind came on the top of the wood in a strong puff, the leaves in front of me burst open, and I saw for a second something hanging in a tree. It was gone in a wink, the puff blowing by and the leaves closing. I tell you the truth; I had made up my mind to see an *aitu*; and if the thing had looked like a pig or a woman, it wouldn't have given me the same turn. The trouble was that it seemed kind of square; and the idea of a square thing that was alive and sang, knocked me sick and silly. I must have stood quite a while; and I made pretty certain it was right out of the same tree that the singing came. Then I began to come to myself a bit.

"Well," says I, "if this is really so, if this is a place where there are square things that sing, I'm gone up anyway. Let's have my fun for my money."

But I thought I might as well take the off-chance of a prayer being any good; so I plumped on my knees and prayed out loud; and all the time I was praying, the strange sounds came out of the tree, and went up and down, and changed, for all the world like music; only you could see it wasn't human—there was nothing there that you could whistle.

As soon as I had made an end in proper style, I laid down my gun, stuck my knife between my teeth, walked right up to that tree, and began to climb. I tell you my heart was like ice. But presently, as I went up, I caught another glimpse of the thing, and that relieved me, for I thought it seemed woundy like a box; and when I had got right up to it, I near fell out of the tree with laughing. A box it was, sure enough, and a candle box at that, with the brand upon the side of it; and it had banjo strings stretched so as to sound when the wind blew. I believe they call the thing a Tyrolean harp, whatever that may mean.

"Well, Mr Case," said I, "you've frightened me once. But I defy you to frighten me again," I says, and slipped down the tree, and set out again to find my enemy's head office, which I guessed would not be far away.

The undergrowth was thick in this part. I couldn't see before my nose, and must burst my way through by main force and ply the knife as I went, slicing the cords of the lianas and slashing down whole trees at a blow. I call them trees for the bigness, but in truth they were just big weeds and sappy to cut through like a carrot. From all this crowd and kind of vegetation, I was just thinking to myself the place might have once been cleared, when I came on my nose over a pile of stones, and saw in a moment it was some kind of a work of man. The Lord knows when it was made or when deserted; for this part of the island has lain undisturbed since long before the whites came. A few steps beyond, I hit into the path I had been always looking for. It was narrow but well beaten, and I saw that Case had plenty of disciples. It seems indeed it was a piece of fashionable boldness to venture up here with the trader; and a young man scarce reckoned himself grown, till he had got his breech tattooed for one thing, and seen Case's devils for another. This is mighty like kanakas; but if you look at it another way, it's mighty like white folks too.

A bit along the path, I was brought to a clean stand and had to rub my eyes. There was a wall in front of me, the path passing it by a gap; it was tumble down and plainly very old, but built of big stones very well laid; and there is no native alive today upon that island that could dream of such a piece of building. Along all the top of it was a line of queer figures, idols, or scare-crows, or what not. They had carved and painted faces, ugly to view; their eyes and teeth were of shell; their hair and their bright clothes blew in the wind, and some of them worked with the tugging. There are islands up west, where they make these kinds of figures till today; but if ever they were made in this island, the practise and the very recollection of it are now long forgotten. And the singular thing was that all these bogies were as fresh as toys out of a shop.

Then it came in my mind what Case had let out to me the first day, that he was a good forger of island curiosities: a thing by which so many traders turn an honest penny. And with that I saw the whole business, and how this display served the man a double purpose: first of all to season his curiosities, and then to frighten those that came to visit him.

But I should tell you (what made the thing more curious) that all the time the Tyrolean harps were harping round me in the trees, and even while I looked a green and yellow bird (that I suppose was building) began to tear the hair off the head of one of the figures.

A little farther on, I found the last curiosity of the museum. The first I saw of it was a longish mound of earth with a twist to it. Digging off the earth with my hands, I found underneath tarpaulin stretched on boards, so that this was plainly the roof of a cellar. It stood right on the top of the hill, and the entrance was on the far side, between two rocks, like the entrance to a cave. I went in as far as the bend, and looking round the corner, saw a shining face. It was big and ugly like a pantomime mask, and the brightness of it waxed and dwindled, and at times it smoked.

"Oho," says I, "luminous paint!"

And I must say I rather admired the man's ingenuity. With a box of tools and a few mighty simple contrivances, he had made out to have a devil of a temple. Any poor kanaka brought up here in the dark, with the harps whining all round him, and shown that smoking face in the bottom of a hole, would make no kind of doubt but he had seen and heard enough devils for a lifetime. It's easy to find out what kanakas think. Just go back to yourself anyway round from ten to fifteen years old, and there's an average kanaka. There are some pious, just as there are pious boys; and the most of them, like the boys again, are middling honest and yet think it rather larks to steal, and are easy scared and rather like to be so. I remembered a boy I was at school with at home, who played the Case business. He didn't know anything, that boy; he couldn't do anything; he had no luminous paint and no Tyrolean harps; he just boldly said he was a sorcerer, and frightened us out of our boots, and we loved it. And then it came in my mind how the master had once flogged that boy, and the surprise we were all in to see the sorcerer catch it and bum like anybody else. Thinks I to myself: "I must find some way of fixing it so for Master Case." And the next moment I had my idea.

I went back by the path which, when once you had found it, was quite plain and easy walking; and when I stepped out on the black sands, who should I see but Master Case himself? I cocked my gun and held it handy; and we marched up and passed without a word, each keeping the tail of his eye on the other; and no sooner had we passed, than we each wheeled round like fellows drilling and stood face to face. We had each taken the same notion in his head, you see, that the other fellow might give him the load of a gun in the stern.

"You've shot nothing," says Case.

"I'm not on the shoot today," says I.

"Well, the devil go with you for me," says he.

"The same to you," says I.

But we stuck just the way we were; no fear of either of us moving. Case laughed. "We can't stop here all day, though," said he.

"Don't let me detain you," says I.

He laughed again. "Look here, Wiltshire, do you think me a fool?" he asked.

"More of a knave if you want to know," says I.

"Well, do you think it would better me to shoot you here on this open beach?" said he, "because I don't. Folks come fishing every day. There may be a score of them up the valley now, making copra; there may be half a dozen on the hill behind you after pigeons; they might be watching us this minute, and I shouldn't wonder. I give you my word I don't want to shoot you. Why should I? You don't hinder me any; you haven't got one pound of copra but what you made with your own hands like a negro slave. You're vegetating, that's what I call it; and I don't care where you vegetate, nor yet how long. Give me your word you don't mean to shoot me, and I'll give you a lead and walk away."

"Well," said I, "you're frank and pleasant, ain't you? and I'll be the same. I don't mean to shoot you today. Why should I? This business is beginning; it ain't done yet, Mr Case. I've given you one turn already, I can see the marks of my knuckles on your head to this blooming hour; and I've more cooking for you. I'm not a paralee like Underhill; my name ain't Adams and it ain't Vigours; and I mean to show you that you've met your match."

"This is a silly way to talk," said he. "This is not the talk to make me move on with."

"All right," said I. "Stay where you are. I ain't in any hurry, and you know it. I can put in the day on this beach, and never mind. I ain't got any copra to bother with. I ain't got any luminous paint to see to."

I was sorry I said that last, but it whipped out before I knew. I could see it took the wind out of his sails, and he stood and stared at me with his brow drawn up. Then I suppose he made up his mind he must get to the bottom of this.

"I take you at your word," says he, and turned his back, and walked right into the devil's bush.

I let him go of course, for I had passed my word. But I watched him as long as he was in sight, and after he was gone, lit out for cover as lively as you would want to see, and went the rest of the way home under the bush. For I didn't trust him sixpenceworth. One thing I saw: I had been ass enough to give him warning; and that which I meant to do, I must do at once.

You would think I had had about enough excitement for one morning; but there was another turn waiting me. As soon as I got far enough round the cape to see my house, I made out there were strangers there; a little farther, and no doubt about it, there were a couple of armed sentries squatting at my door. I could only suppose the trouble about Uma must have come to a head, and the station been seized. For aught I could think Uma was taken up already, and these armed men were waiting to do the like by me.

However, as I came nearer, which I did at top speed, I saw there was a third native sitting on the verandah like a guest, and Uma was talking with him like a hostess. Nearer still I made out it was the big young chief Maea, and that he was smiling away and smoking; and what was he smoking?—none of your European cigarettes fit for a cat; not even the genuine, big, knock-me-down native article, that a fellow can really put in the time with, if his pipe is broke; but a cigar, and one of my Mexicans at that, that I could swear to. At sight of this, my heart started beating; and I took a wild hope in my head that the trouble was over, and Maea had come round.

Uma pointed me out to him, as I came up, and he met me at the head of my own stairs like a thorough gentleman.

"Vilivili," said he, which was the best they could make of my name, "I pleased."

There is no doubt when an island chief wants to be civil he can do it. I saw the way things were from the word go. There was no call for Uma to say to me: "He no 'fraid Ese now; come bring copra." I tell you I shook hands with that kanaka like as if he was the best white man in Europe.

The fact was Case and he had got after the same girl, or Maea suspected it and concluded to make hay of the trader on the chance. He had dressed himself up, got a couple of his retainers cleaned and armed to kind of make the thing more public, and just waiting till Case was clear of the village, came round to put the whole of his business my way. He was rich as well as powerful, I suppose that man was worth fifty thousand nuts per annum. I gave him the price of the beach and a quarter cent better, and as for credit, I would have advanced him the inside of the store and the fittings besides, I was so pleased to see him. I must say he bought like a gentleman: rice and tins and biscuit enough for a week's feast, and stuffs by the bolt. He was agreeable besides; he had plenty fun to him; and we cracked jests together, mostly through Uma for interpreter, because he had mighty little English, and my native was still off colour. One thing I made out: he could never really have thought much harm of Uma; he could never have been really frightened, and must just have made believe from dodginess and because he thought Case had a strong pull in the village and could help him on.

This set me thinking that both he and I were in a tightish place. What he had done was to fly in the face of the whole village, and the thing might cost him his authority. More than that, after my talk with Case on the beach, I thought it might very well cost me my life. Case had as good as said he would pot me if ever I got copra; he would come home to find the best business in the village had changed hands; and the best thing I thought I could do was to get in first with the potting.

"See here, Uma," says I, "tell him I'm sorry I made him wait, but I was looking at Case's Tiapolo store in the bush."

"He want savvy if you no 'fraid?" translated Uma.

I laughed out. "Not much!" says I. "Tell him the place is a blooming toyshop! Tell him in England we give these things to the kids to play with."

"He want savvy if you hear devil sing?" she asked next.

"Look here," I said, "I can't do it now because I've got no banjo strings in stock; but the next time the ship comes round, I'll have one of these same contraptions right here in my verandah, and he can see for himself how much devil there is to it. Tell him, as soon as I can get the strings, I'll make one for his picaninnies. The name of the concern is a Tyrolean harp; and you can tell him the name means in English, that nobody but damfools give a cent for it."

This time he was so pleased he had to try his English again. "You talk true?" says he.

"Rather!" said I. "Talk all-e-same bible. Bring out a bible here, Uma, if you've got such a thing, and I'll kiss it. Or I'll tell you what's better still," says I, taking a header. "Ask him if he's afraid to go up there himself by day."

It appeared he wasn't; he could venture as far as that by day and in company.

"That's the ticket, then!" said I. "Tell him the man's a fraud and the place foolishness, and if he'll go up there tomorrow, he'll see all that's left of it. But tell him this, Uma, and mind he understands it; if he gets talking, it's bound to come to Case and I'm a dead man. I'm playing his game, tell him, and if he says one word, my blood will be at his door and be the damnation of him here and after."

She told him, and he shook hands with me up to the hilts, and says he: "No talk. Go up tomollow. You my friend?"

"No, sir!" says I. "No such foolishness. I've come here to trade, tell him, and not to make friends. But as to Case, I'll send that man to glory."

So off Maea went, pretty well pleased, as I could see.

Chapter V

Night in the Bush

Well, I was committed now; Tiapolo had to be smashed up before next day; and my hands were pretty full, not only with preparations, but with argument. My house was like a mechanics' debating society; Uma was so made up that I shouldn't go into the bush by night, or that if I did I was never to come back again. You know her style of arguing, you've had a specimen about Queen Victoria and the devil; and I leave you to fancy if I was tired of it before dark.

At last, I had a good idea; what was the use of casting my pearls before her? I thought: some of her own chopped hay would be likelier to do the business.

"I'll tell you what, then," said I. "You fish out your bible, and I'll take that up along with me. That'll make me right."

She swore a bible was no use.

"That's just your blamed kanaka ignorance," said I. "Bring the bible out."

She brought it, and I turned to the title page where I thought there would likely be some English, and so there was. "There!" said I. "Look at that! '*London: printed for the British and Foreign Bible Society, Blackfriars*'; and the date, which I can't read, owing to its being in these X's. There's no devil in hell can look near the Bible Society, Blackfriars. Why, you silly!" I said, "how do you suppose we get along with our own *aitus* at home? All Bible Society!"

"I think you no got any," said she. "White man he tell me you no got."

"Sounds likely, don't it?" I asked. "Why would these islands all be chock full of them, and none in Europe?"

"Well, you no got breadfruit," said she.

I could have tore my hair. "Now, look here, old lady," said I, "you dry up, for I'm tired of you. I'll take the bible, which'll put me as straight as the mail; and that's the last word I've got to say."

The night fell extraordinary dark, clouds coming up with sundown and overspreading all; not a star showed; there was only an end of a moon, and that not due before the small hours. Round the village, what with the lights and the fires in the open houses and the torches of many fishers moving on the reef, it kept as gay as an illumination; but the sea and the mountains and woods were all clean gone. I suppose it might be eight o'clock when I took the road, loaden like a donkey. First there was that bible, a book as big as your head, which I had let myself in for by my own tomfoolery. Then there was my gun and knife and lantern and patent matches, all necessary. And then there was the real plant of the affair in hand, a mortal weight of gunpowder, a pair of dynamite fishing-bombs, and two or three pieces of slow match that I had hauled out of the tin cases and spliced together the best way I could; for the match was only trade stuff, and a man would be crazy that trusted it. Altogether, you see, I had the materials of a pretty good blow up. Expense was nothing to me; I wanted that thing done right.

As long as I was in the open, and had the lamp in my house to steer by, I did well. But when I got to the path, it fell so dark I could make no headway, walking into trees and swearing there, like a man looking for the matches in his bedroom. I knew it was risky to light up; for my lantern would be visible all the way to the point of the cape; and as no one went there after dark, it would be talked about and come to Case's ears. But what was I to do? I had either to give the business over and lose caste with Maea, or light up, take my chance, and get through the thing the smartest I was able.

As long as I was on the path, I walked hard; but when I came to the black beach, I had to run. For the tide was now nearly flowed; and to get through with my powder dry between the surf and the steep hill, took all the quickness I possessed. As it was even, the wash caught me to the knees and I came near falling on a stone. All this time, the hurry I was in, and the free air and smell of the sea, kept my spirits lively; but when I was once in the bush and began to climb the path, I took it easier. The fearsomeness of the wood had been a good bit rubbed off for me by Master Case's banjo strings and graven images; yet I thought it was a dreary walk, and guessed, when the disciples went up there, they must be badly scared. The light of the lantern, striking among all these trunks, and forked branches, and twisted rope's-ends of lianas, made the whole place, or all that you could see it, a kind of a puzzle of turning shadows. They came to meet you, solid and quick like giants, and then span off and vanished; they hove up over your head like clubs, and flew away into the night like birds. The floor of the bush glim-mered with dead wood, the way the matchbox used to shine after you had struck a lucifer. Big cold drops fell on me from the branches overhead like sweat. There was no wind to mention, only a little icy breath of a land breeze that stirred nothing; and the harps were silent.

The first landfall I made was when I got through the bush of wild cocoanuts, and came in view of the bogies on the wall. Mighty queer they looked by the shining of the lantern, with their painted faces, and shell eyes, and their clothes and their hair hanging. One after another I pulled them all up and piled them in a bundle on the cellar roof, so as they might go to glory with the rest. Then I chose a place behind one of the big stones at the entrance, buried my powder and the two shells, and arranged my match along the passage. And then I had a look at the smoking head, just for good-bye. It was doing fine.

"Cheer up," says I. "You're booked."

It was my first idea to light up and be getting homeward; for the darkness, and the glimmer of the dead wood, and the shadows of the lantern made me lonely. But I knew where one of the harps hung; it seemed a pity it shouldn't go with the rest; and at the same time I couldn't help letting on to myself that I was mortal tired of my employment and would like best to be at home and have the door shut. I stepped out of the cellar, and argued it fore and back. There was a sound of the sea far down below me on the coast; nearer hand, not a leaf stirred; I might have been the only living creature this side Cape Horn. Well, as I stood there thinking, it seemed the bush woke and became full of little noises. Little noises they were, and nothing to hurt—a bit of a crackle, a bit of a brush—but the breath jumped right out of me and my throat went as dry as a biscuit. It wasn't Case I was afraid of, which would have been common sense; I never thought of Case; what took me, as sharp as the cholic, was the old wives' tales, the devil-women and the man-pigs. It was the toss of a penny whether I should run; but I got a purchase on myself, and stepped out, and held up the lantern (like a fool) and looked all round.

In the direction of the village and the path, there was nothing to be seen; but when I turned inland, it's a wonder to me I didn't drop. There—coming right up out of the desert and the bad bush—there, sure enough, was a devil-woman, just the way I had figured she would look. I saw the light shine on her bare arms and her bright eyes. And there went out of me a yell so big that I thought it was my death.

"Ah! No sing out!" says the devil-woman, in a kind of a high whisper. "Why you talk big voice? Put out light! Ese he come."

"My God Almighty, Uma, is that you?" says I.

"Ioe," says she. "I come quick. Ese here soon."

"You come alone?" I asked. "You no 'fraid?"

"Ah, too much 'fraid!" she whispered, clutching me. "I think die."

"Well," says I, with a kind of a weak grin, "I'm not the one to laugh at you, Mrs Wiltshire, for I'm about the worst scared man in the South Pacific myself."

She told me in two words what brought her. I was scarce gone, it seems, when Faavao came in; and the old woman had met Black Jack running as hard as he was fit from our house to Case's. Uma

neither spoke nor stopped, but lit right out to come and warn me.
She was so close at my heels that the lantern was her guide across
the beach, and afterwards, by the glimmer of it in the trees, she
got her line up hill. It was only when I had got to the top or was in
the cellar, that she wandered—Lord knows where!—and lost a
sight of precious time, afraid to call out lest Case was at the heels
of her, and falling in the bush so that she was all knocked and
bruised. That must have been when she got too far to the south-
ward, and how she came to take me in the flank at last, and
frighten me beyond what I've got the words to tell of.

Well, anything was better than a devil-woman; but I thought
her yarn serious enough. Black Jack had no call to be about my
house, unless he was set there to watch; and it looked to me as if
my tomfool word about the paint and perhaps some chatter of
Maea's had got us all in a clove hitch. One thing was clear: Uma
and I were here for the night; we daren't try to go home before day,
and even then it would be safer to strike round up the mountain
and come in by the back of the village, or we might walk into an
ambuscade. It was plain too that the mine should be sprung immediately, or Case might be in time to stop it.

I marched into the tunnel, Uma keeping tight hold of me,
opened my lantern and lit the match. The first length of it burned
like a spill of paper; and I stood stupid, watching it burn, and
thinking we were going aloft with Tiapolo, which was none of my
views. The second took to a better rate, though faster than I cared
about; and at that I got my wits again, hauled Uma clear of the
passage, blew out and dropped the lantern; and the pair of us
groped our way into the bush until I thought it might be safe, and
lay down together by a tree.

"Old lady," I said, "I won't forget this night. You're a trump, and
that's what's wrong with you."

She humped herself close up to me. She had run out the way
she was with nothing on but her kilt; and she was all wet with the
dews and the sea on the black beach, and shook straight on with
cold and the terror of the dark and the devils.

"Too much 'fraid," was all she said.

The far side of Case's hill goes down near as steep as a precipice into the next valley. We were on the very edge of it, and I could see the dead wood shine and hear the sea sound far below. I didn't care about the position, which left me no retreat, but I was afraid to change. Then I saw I had made a worse mistake about the lantern, which I should have left lighted, so that I could have had a crack at Case when he stepped into the shine of it. And even if I hadn't had the wit to do that, it seemed a senseless thing to leave the good lantern to blow up with the graven images; the thing belonged to me, after all, and was worth money, and might come in handy. If I could have trusted the match, I might have run in still and rescued it. But who was going to trust the match? You know what trade is; the stuff was good enough for kanakas to go fishing with, where they've got to look lively anyway, and the most they risk is only to have their hand blown off; but for any one that wanted to fool around a blow-up like mine, that match was rubbish.

Altogether, the best I could do was to lie still, see my shot gun handy, and wait for the explosion. But it was a solemn kind of a business; the blackness of the night was like solid; the only thing you could see was the nasty, bogy glimmer of the dead wood, and that showed you nothing but itself; and as for sounds, I stretched my ears till I thought I could have heard the match burn in the tunnel, and that bush was as silent as a coffin. Now and then there was a bit of a crack, but whether it was near or far, whether it was Case stubbing his toes within a few yards of me or a tree breaking miles away, I knew no more than the babe unborn.

And then all of a sudden Vesuvius went off. It was a long time coming; but when it came (though I say it that shouldn't) no man could ask to see a better. At first it was just a son of a gun of a row, and a spout of fire, and the wood lighted up so that you could see to read. And then the trouble began. Uma and I were half buried under a waggonful of earth, and glad it was no worse; for one of the rocks at the entrance of the tunnel was fired clean into the air, fell within a couple of fathom of where we lay, and bounded over the edge of the hill, and went pounding down into the next valley.

I saw I had rather under-calculated our distance, or overdone the dynamite and powder, which you please.

And presently I saw I had made another slip. The noise of the thing began to die off, shaking the island; the dazzle was over; and yet the night didn't come back the way that I expected. For the whole wood was scattered with red coals and brands from the explosion; they were all round me on the flat, some had fallen below in the valley, and some stuck and flared in the treetops. I had no fear of fire, for these forests are too wet to kindle. But the trouble was that the place was all lit up, not very bright but good enough to get a shot by; and the way the coals were scattered, it was just as likely Case might have the advantage as myself. I looked all round for his white face, you may be sure; but there was not a sign of him. As for Uma, the life seemed to have been knocked right out of her by the bang and blaze of it.

There was one bad point in my game. One of the blessed graven images had come down all afire, hair and clothes and body, not four yards away from me. I cast a mighty noticing glance all round; there was still no Case; and I made up my mind I must get rid of that burning stick before he came, or I should be shot there like a dog.

It was my first idea to have crawled; and then I thought speed was the main thing, and stood half up to make a rush. The same moment, from somewhere between me and the sea, there came a flash and a report, and a rifle bullet screeched in my ear. I swung straight round, and up with my gun. But the brute had a Winchester; and before I could as much as see him, his second shot knocked me over like a ninepin. I seemed to fly in the air, then came down by the run and lay half a minute silly; and then I found my hands empty and my gun had flown over my head as I fell. It makes a man mighty wide awake to be in the kind of box that I was in. I scarce knew where I was hurt, or whether I was hurt or not, but turned right over on my face to crawl after my weapon. Unless you have tried to get about with a smashed leg, you don't know what pain is, and I let a howl out like a bullock's.

This was the unluckiest noise that ever I made in my life. Up to then, Uma had stuck to her tree like a sensible woman, knowing she would be only in the way. But as soon as she heard me sing out, she ran forward—the Winchester cracked again—and down she went.

I had sat up, leg and all, to stop her; but when I saw her tumble, I clapped down again where I was, lay still, and felt the handle of my knife. I had been scurried and put out before. No more of that for me; he had knocked over my girl, I had got to fix him for it; and I lay there and gritted my teeth, and footed up the chances. My leg was broke, my gun was gone, Case had still ten shots in his Winchester, it looked a kind of hopeless business. But I never despaired nor thought upon despairing: that man had got to go.

For a goodish bit, not one of us let on. Then I heard Case begin to move nearer in the bush, but mighty careful. The image had burned out; there were only a few coals left here and there; and the wood was main dark, but had a kind of a low glow in it like a fire on its last legs. It was by this that I made out Case's head looking at me over a big tuft of ferns; and at the same time the brute saw me and shouldered his Winchester. I lay quite still and as good as looked into the barrel; it was my last chance; but I thought my heart would have come right out of its bearings. Then he fired. Lucky for me it was no shot gun, for the bullet struck within an inch of me and knocked the dirt in my eyes.

Just you try and see if you can lie quiet, and let a man take a sitting shot at you, and miss you by a hair! But I did, and lucky too. Awhile Case stood with the Winchester at the port-arms; then he gave a little laugh to himself, and stepped round the ferns.

"Laugh!" thought I. "If you had the wit of a louse, you would be praying!"

I was all as taut as a ship's hauser or the spring of a watch; and as soon as he came within reach of me, I had him by the ankle, plucked the feet right out from under him, laid him out, and was upon the top of him, broken leg and all, before he breathed. His Winchester had gone the same road as my shot gun; it was nothing to me; I defied him now. I'm a pretty strong man anyway, but I never knew what strength was till I got hold of Case. He was knocked out of time by the rattle he came down with, and threw up his hands together, more like a frightened woman, so that I caught both of them with my left. This wakened him up, and he fixed his teeth in my forearm like a weasel. Much I cared! My leg gave me all the pain I had any use for; and I drew my knife, and got it in the place.

"Now," said I, "I've got you; and you're gone up, and a good job too. Do you feel the point of that? That's for Underhill. And there's for Adams. And now here's for Uma, and that's going to knock your blooming soul right out of you."

With that, I gave him the cold steel for all I was worth. His body kicked under me like a spring sofa; he gave a dreadful kind of a long moan, and lay still.

"I wonder if you're dead. I hope so," I thought, for my head was swimming. But I wasn't going to take chances; I had his own example too close before me for that; and I tried to draw the knife out to give it him again. The blood came over my hands, I remember, hot as tea; and with that I fainted clean away and fell with my head on the man's mouth.

When I came to myself, it was pitch dark; the cinders had burned out, there was nothing to be seen but the shine of the dead wood; and I couldn't remember where I was, nor why I was in such pain, nor what I was all wetted with. Then it came back; and the first thing I attended to was to give him the knife again a half a dozen times up to the handle. I believe he was dead already; but it did him no harm and did me good.

"I bet you're dead now," I said, and then I called to Uma.

Nothing answered; and I made a move to go and grope for her, fouled my broken leg, and fainted again.

When I came to myself the second time, the clouds had all cleared away except a few that sailed there, white as cotton. The moon was up, a tropic moon. The moon at home turns a wood black; but even this old but-end of a one showed up that forest as green as by day. The night birds—or rather they're a kind of early morning bird—sang out with their long, falling notes like nightingales. And I could see the dead man that I was still half resting on, looking right up into the sky with his open eyes, no paler than when he was alive; and a little way off, Uma tumbled on her side. I got over to her the best way I was able; and when I got there, she was broad awake and crying and sobbing to herself with no more noise than an insect. It appears she was afraid to cry out loud, because of the *aitus*. Altogether she was not much hurt, but scared beyond belief; she had come to her senses a long while ago, cried out to me, heard nothing in reply, made out we were both dead, and had lain there ever since, afraid to budge a finger. The ball had ploughed up her shoulder; and she had lost a main quantity of blood; but I soon had that tied up the way it ought to be with the tail of my shirt and a scarf I had on, got her head on my sound knee and my back against a trunk, and settled down to wait for morning. Uma was for neither use nor ornament; and could only clutch hold of me, and shake, and cry; I don't suppose there was ever anybody worse scared, and to do her justice, she had had a lively night of it. As for me, I was in a good bit of pain and fever, but not so bad when I sat still; and every time I looked over to Case, I could have sung and whistled. Talk about meat and drink! to see that man lying there dead as a herring filled me full.

The night birds stopped after a while; and then the light began to change, the east came orange, the whole wood began to whirr with singing like a musical box, and there was the broad day.

I didn't expect Maea for a long while yet; and indeed I thought there was an off chance he might go back on the whole idea and not come at all. I was the better pleased when, about an hour after daylight, I heard sticks smashing and a lot of kanakas laughing and singing out to keep their courage up. Uma sat up quite brisk at the first word of it; and presently we saw a party come stringing out of the path, Maea in front and behind him a white man in a pith helmet. It was Mr Tarleton who had turned up late last night in Falesá, having left his boat and walked the last stage with a lantern.

They buried Case upon the field of glory, right in the hole where he had kept the smoking head. I waited till the thing was done; and Mr Tarleton prayed, which I thought tomfoolery, but I'm

bound to say he gave a pretty sick view of the dear departed's pros-
pects, and seemed to have his own ideas of hell. I had it out with
him afterwards, told him he had scamped his duty, and what he
had ought to have done was to up like a man and tell the kanakas
plainly Case was damned, and a good riddance; but I never could
get him to see it my way. Then they made me a litter of poles and
carried me down to the station. Mr Tarleton set my leg, and made
a regular missionary splice of it, so that I limp to this day. That
done, he took down my evidence, and Uma's, and Maea's, wrote
it all out fair, and had us sign it; and then he got the chiefs and
marched over to Papa Randall's to seize Case's papers.

All they found was a bit of a diary, kept for a good many years,
and all about the price of copra and chickens being stolen and that;
and the books of the business, and the will I told you of in the
beginning, by both of which the whole thing (stock lock and barrel) appeared to belong to the Sāmoa woman. It was I that bought
her out, at a mighty reasonable figure, for she was in a hurry to get
home. As for Randall and the black, they had to tramp; got into
some kind of a station on the Papa-mālūlū side; did very bad business, for the truth is neither of the pair was fit for it; and lived
mostly on fish, which was the means of Randall's death. It seems
there was a nice shoal in one day, and papa went after them with
dynamite; either the match burned too fast or papa was full, or
both, but the shell went off (in the usual way) before he threw it;
and where was papa's hand? Well, there's nothing to hurt in that;
the islands up north are all full of one-handed men, like the parties
in the Arabian Nights; but either Randall was too old, or he drank
too much, and the short and the long of it was that he died. Pretty
soon after, the nigger was turned out of the islands for stealing from
white men, and went off to the west, where he found men of his
own colour, in case he liked that, and the men of his own colour
took and ate him at some kind of a corroborree and I'm sure I hope
he was to their fancy!

So there was I left alone in my glory at Falesá; and when the
schooner came round I filled her up and gave her a deck cargo half

as high as the house. I must say Mr Tarleton did the right thing by us; but he took a meanish kind of a revenge.

"Now, Mr Wiltshire," said he, "I've put you all square with everybody here. It wasn't difficult to do, Case being gone; but I have done it, and given my pledge besides that you will deal fairly with the natives. I must ask you to keep my word."

Well, so I did. I used to be bothered about my balances; but I reasoned it out this way. We all have queerish balances, and the natives all know it and water their copra in a proportion; so that it's fair all round. But the truth is, it did use to bother me; and though I did well in Falesá, I was half-glad when the firm moved me on to another station, where I was under no kind of a pledge, and could look my balances in the face.

As for the old lady, you know her as well as I do. She's only the one fault: if you don't keep your eye lifting, she would give away the roof off the station. Well, it seems it's natural in kanakas. She's turned a powerful big woman now, and could throw a London bobby over her shoulder. But that's natural in kanakas too; and there's no manner of doubt that she's an A one wife.

Mr Tarleton's gone home, his trick being over; he was the best missionary I ever struck, and now it seems he's parsonizing down Somerset ways. Well, that's best for him; he'll have no kanakas there to get luny over.

My public house? Not a bit of it, nor ever likely; I'm stuck here, I fancy; I don't like to leave the kids, you see; and there's no use talking—they're better here than what they would be in a white man's country. Though Ben took the eldest up to Auckland, where he's being schooled with the best. But what bothers me is the girls. They're only half castes of course; I know that as well as you do, and there's nobody thinks less of half castes than I do; but they're mine, and about all I've got; I can't reconcile my mind to their taking up with kanakas, and I'd like to know where I'm to find them whites?

Glossary

Glossary

Stevenson's later style was recognized immediately by his contemporaries for its newness. "The slang of the Pacific," remarked a reviewer of *The Wrecker* in 1892, "is used with such freedom that we should now and then be grateful for a concise glossary." What follows is designed to make clear the meaning of words and phrases that might be unintelligible to a modern reader: English and American slang, archaisms, nautical terms. Definitions are largely drawn from nineteenth-century dictionaries of slang and Americanisms. They convey the flavor of the period and frequently enable us to see how Stevenson manipulated the language for his own ends. Unless otherwise noted, the following texts serve as the sources for the definitions:

AF   Alexander Findlay, *A Directory for the Navigation of the South Pacific Ocean* (5th ed., London, 1884).

B&L   Albert Barrère and Charles G. Leland, *A Dictionary of Slang, Jargon & Cant* (2 vols., London, 1897).

BJT   B. J. Totten, *Naval Text-Book . . . and A Marine Dictionary* (Boston, 1841).

F&H   J. S. Farmer and W. E. Henley, *Slang and Its Analogues* (7 vols., London, 1890–1904).

JCH   John Camden Hotten, *The Slang Dictionary: A New Edition* (London, 1874).

JRB   John Russell Bartlett, *Dictionary of Americanisms* (4th ed., Boston, 1884).

JSF   J. S. Farmer, *Americanisms* (London, 1889).

JW   Joseph Wright, *The English Dialect Dictionary* (6 vols., Oxford, 1898–1905).

MS   The manuscript of *The Beach of Falesá*.

NE   *A Naval Encyclopedia* (Philadelphia, 1881).

SdV   M. Schele de Vere, *Americanisms* (New York, 1872).

WCR   W. Clark Russell, *Sailors' Language* (London, 1883).

WHS   William Henry Smyth, *The Sailor's Word-Book* (London, 1867).

W 1890 *An American Dictionary of the English Language* (Springfield, Mass., 1890). [Webster's.]

[The numbers in the following section are page and line numbers.]

27.7 *line*
The equator (WCR).

28.4 *stick*
Familiar phrase for mast (WHS).

28.4 *John Adams, obit eighteen and sixty eight*
One of Stevenson's invaluable sources for Pacific materials was Alexander Findlay's *Directory* (AF). The novelist wrote to Charles Baxter in early April 1890: "Persons with friends in the islands should purchase Findlay's *Pacific Directories*: they're the best of reading anyway, and may almost count as fiction" (DeLancey Ferguson and Marshall Waingrow, eds., *R. L. S.: Stevenson's Letters to Charles Baxter* [New Haven, Conn., 1956], p. 267). Stevenson's copy, probably purchased for him by S. S. McClure in New York City, had "Stevenson" written in ink across the top of the more than 1,250 pages. Stevenson drew on details from the Samoan section (pp. 653–69) for *Falesá*: "Between the years 1868 and 1873, and again in 1879–80, these islands were devastated by a civil war, but in 1882 the country appeared to be much more settled, under the rule of King Malietoa Laupepa. . . . The Pilot for Pago-Pago lives on the island of Anuu. . . . His name is John Adams, a native of the Sandwich Islands. He has been here about ten years, and speaks English sufficiently well to make himself understood (1876)."

28.9 *Pain-Killer and Kennedy's Discovery*
Pain-Killer was a nostrum made at Providence, R.I., by Perry Davis & Son; it was as popular in India, China, Japan, and Europe, as it was in the United States (JRB). "Dr. Donald Kennedy advanced a bloodhound theory of medicine. 'My Medical Discovery,' he advertised, 'seldom takes hold of two people alike! Why? Because no two people have the same weak spot. Beginning at the stomach, it goes searching through the body for any hidden humor. . . . Perhaps it's only a little sediment left on a nerve or in a gland; the Medical Discovery slides it right along, and you find quick happiness from the first bottle. Perhaps it's a big sediment or open sore, well settled somewhere, ready to fight. The Medical Discovery begins this fight, and you think it pretty hard; but soon you thank me for making something that has reached your weak spot.'" (James Young, *The Toadstool Millionaires* [Princeton, N.J., 1961], p. 170.) Dr. Ashbel P. Grinnell, a New York physician who made a statistical study of patent medicines, asserted that more alcohol was consumed in the United States in patent medicines than was dispensed legally by licensed liquor vendors, barring the sale of ales and beer (Samuel Hopkins Adams, "Peruna and the Bracers," reprinted from *Collier's Weekly*, October 28, 1905, in his *The Great American Fraud* [New York, 1905], p. 12).

28.20 *Black Jack*
A black-jack was a piratical-looking individual or the ensign of a pirate (NE). The term could also refer to a capacious tin can for beer (WHS).

28.20 *Whistling Jimmy*
A whistling-shop was a place where spirits were sold without a license (JCH).

28.26 *pass*
A geographical term abbreviated from passage; also, any difficult strait that commands the entrance into a country (WHS). "While the trade wind is blowing vessels may anchor off the village of *Feleasau*, in a small bay just East of the N.W. point of the island [of Manua]. . . . The landing place is a very narrow passage through the reef, only wide enough for a whale boat, and is dangerous if there is much swell on." (AF.)

28.27 *stern sheets*
The after part of an open boat (WCR), often furnished with seats to accommodate passengers (BJT).

28.31 *gallows*
An intensifier signifying very or exceedingly (JCH).

29.21 *kanaka*
Hawaiian term for man; also used pejoratively to signify a native (Lorrin Andrews, *A Dictionary of the Hawaiian Language* [Honolulu, 1865], p. 256).

29.32 *Manu'a*
Manua is the easternmost group of islands of the principal range of Samoan islands (AF).

29.32 *does*
To get on, grow, thrive, flourish (JW).

30.9 *get his shirt out*
Get angry (F&H).

30.14 *Miller a Dutchman*
Sailors often called all northern Europeans "Dutchmen" (WCR).

30.30 *a labour ship*
"The labor traffic, or blackbirding, as it was called by its apologists and its enemies respectively, rivalled the cruelties of the Middle Passage of the African slave trade. . . . The labor is recruited from the unsettled islands of the Western Pacific, from the Solomons and other groups down about New Guinea. Ships are sent recruiting, a formal contract is entered into with each man to labor for three years at a fixed rate, probably a dollar a month and his rations and clothing, payment to be made at the end of his term of service in goods and a box to put them in, the laborer to be returned to the exact place from which he was taken. Only a house with large resources and extensive need for labor can engage profitably in this traffic, therefore all the field labor, the 'black boys,' have been handled in Samoa through one house, which is under direct governmental supervision. These are the men who do the actual work, who cut the copra and dry it, who do not ask more than a dollar a month as wages for an unlimited amount of work, and who never shirk their jobs. The black boy is . . . a dogged worker and the mainspring of whatever industry there is in

Samoa." (Llewella Pierce Churchill, *Samoa 'Uma* [New York, 1902], pp. 233–34.)

31.12 *Fiddler's Green*
A sort of sensual Elysium, the place where sailors expect to go when they die (WHS). It is a place of fiddling, dancing, rum, and tobacco (JCH).

31.29 *cutty stark*
A short or scanty chemise (JCH).

32.19 *the cut of your jib*
The expression on one's face (WHS).

32.23 *to hurt*
To matter, signify (JW).

33.12 *full*
Drunk. (F&H)

33.21 *old man*
The term applied to the captain by a crew (WCR).

33.25 *Dry up*
Hush; be quiet (JSF).

34.13 *old gentleman*
The devil (JCH).

35.11 *Hard-shell Baptis'*
"Originally sects of the Baptist denomination were termed *Hard-shells* and *Soft-shells*, by their unregenerate critics" (JSF). "*Hard Shell Baptists*, who call themselves *Primitive* Baptists, set their faces like flint—to use their own term—against an educated ministry, and especially against all foreign evangelical missions" (SdV).

39.9 *mortal*
An intensifier signifying extremely or great (JW).

40.5 *shipshape and Bristol fashion*
A reference to Bristol in its palmy commercial days, before it was superseded by Liverpool as the chief port on the western side of England (WHS).

40.8 *Devil a wink*
An indefinite intensifier: e.g., devil of a mess, devil of a woman, devil of a row (F&H).

41.33 *Ben*
In the spring of 1890 Stevenson left Sydney for a roundabout voyage to Samoa in "the steamship *Janet Nicoll*, an iron screw-steamer of about six hundred tons, chartered by Messrs. Henderson and Macfarlane, a well-known South Sea firm. There was a dock strike in Sydney at the time, but with a 'blackboy' crew on board, the *Janet* got away, carrying a full complement of officers and engineers, and the trio to whom *Island Nights' Entertainments* was afterwards dedicated—Mr. Henderson, one of the partners; Ben Hird, the supercargo;

and 'Jack' Buckland, the living original of Tommy Haddon in *The Wrecker*." (Graham Balfour, *The Life of Robert Louis Stevenson* [London, 1901], II, 90.)

43.11 *fussy-ocky*
Fasioti is a verb meaning to kill someone (George Pratt, *A Grammar and Dictionary of the Samoan Language* [2d ed., ed. S. J. Whitmee, London, 1878], p. 191).

44.11 *Buncombe*
Bunkum, or talking merely for talk's sake. The original use of the word in this sense is ascribed to Felix Walker, a congressman from Buncombe County, North Carolina, who explained that he was merely talking "Buncombe" when his fellow members could not understand why he was making a speech. "That's all *buncombe*" is equivalent to "that's all nonsense, or an absurdity" (JSF).

44.14 *cure*
A contemptuous term for an odd person; abridged from "curiosity" (JCH). More generally, a humorous, comical person (B&L).

44.35 *horrors*
Delirium tremens (B&L).

45.5 *taking*
Agitation; excitement; distress of mind (W 1890). A fit of petulance or temper (JW).

45.5 *Johnny had slipped his cable*
To "slip the cable" means to let go of the inboard end and allow the entire cable to run out (NE).

45.12 *slanging*
Abusing in foul language (JCH).

45.16 *goods*
"Among the Molly Maguires . . . the signs and pass-words constituted the *goods* of the society. The same usage applies in the case of other secret organizations." (JSF).

46.21 *buck*
A term often vulgarly applied to a Negro man (JRB).

46.31 *struck all of a heap*
Suddenly astonished (JCH).

49.4 *sawder*
"Soft sawder" is obvious flattery (JSF).

49.14 *to come any of their native ideas over me*
"To come over" or "come it over one" is a vulgar expression for getting the advantage of someone (JRB).

49.25 *put my monkey up*
Rouse one's passion or ill temper (JCH).

50.23 *down*
Suspicion; alarm (F&H).

51.28 *bacon*
Body (JCH).

53.19 *mummy apple*
"The Mammee Apple, which grows well in Hawaii, is a native of the West Indies, and is a fruit much esteemed in tropical countries. . . . The fruit may be eaten raw, and is very delicious when preserved." (Gerrit P. Wilder, *Fruits of the Hawaiian Islands* [Honolulu, 1911], p. 60.)

55.28 *Beach de Mar*
The jargon or "pidgin" of the Western Pacific. According to William Churchill, the term "Beach-la-mar" derived from a common sailor mispronunciation of *bêche-de-mer*, a name given to the edible trepang, or sea cucumber (*Beach-la-Mar: The Jargon or Trade Speech of the Western Pacific* [Washington, D.C., 1911], p. 4).

56.4 *meat and drink*
Strong drink; also liquor thickened with egg yolks (F&H).

56.7 *beachcomber*
A long wave rolling in from the ocean (W 1890). Also, a contemptuous term for someone who hangs about the shore on the lookout for jobs; chiefly applied to runaway seamen and deserters from whalers who lived along the beaches in South America and in the South Sea islands (WCR).

56.11 *Apia and Papeete*
"The other port centres of the Pacific Islands exerted a similar [demoralizing] influence. The beachcombers of Tahiti concentrated in Papeete. It became one of the favourite provisioning centres for whalers. Of course when rowdy ships came in, it was difficult to preserve order. The place got, however, a worse name than it ever deserved. Apia in Samoa was known as the Hell of the Pacific until the 1870's." (Aarne A. Koskinen, *Missionary Influence as a Political Factor in the Pacific Islands* [Helsinki, 1953], p. 130.)

56.11 *flash*
Low and vulgar (W 1890); pertaining to thieves and criminals (F&H).

56.12 *Fale-alii*
"At 8 miles beyond Safatu is *Falealili Harbour*, very small, and obstructed by outlying reefs; there is a large native town here" (AF).

56.26 *Ioe*
"Yes" (MS).

57.18 *cut up downright rough*
Become obstreperous and dangerous (JCH).

57.32 *sweep*
A contemptuous term for a low or shabby man (JCH).

60.31 *bunged*
Threw with force (JW).

62.32 *Aué*
"Alas!" (MS).

65.18 *flying*
Circulating as a tale or rumor, without definite authority (NED).

70.6 *buffer*
A term for a good-humored or liberal old man (JCH).

70.22 *big don and the funny dog*
"'Don' . . . An adept; a swell. 'Dog' . . . A man; sometimes used contemptuously." (F&H).

71.12 *Obstropulous*
A New England corruption of "obstreperous" (JRB).

71.18 *pot-hunting*
"Pot-hunter, a sportsman who shoots anything he comes across, having more regard to filling his bag than to the rules which regulate the sport" (JCH).

75.36 *skylarked*
Originally, to mount the mast and slide down the stays for amusement (WHS); to engage in horseplay or act the fool (WCR).

76.4 *cracked on*
Added sail in a strong wind (WCR).

77.23 *lots of sensitive*
"Right in the wild lime hedge which cuts athwart us just homeward of the garden, I found a great bed of kuikui—sensitive plant—our deadliest enemy. A fool brought it to this island in a pot, and used to lecture and sentimentalise over the tender thing. The tender thing has now taken charge of this island, and men fight it, with torn hands, for bread and life. A singular, insidious thing, shrinking and biting like a weasel; clutching by its roots as a limpet clutches to a rock." (Robert Louis Stevenson, *Vailima Letters* [London, 1895], pp. 13–14.)

79.15 *gone up*
Gone to heaven (SdV); dead (JSF).

79.27 *woundy*
An intensifier signifying "extremely" or "excessively," this word never appeared in any edition of *Falesá*. Branded "a low bad word" by Johnson, and clearly a term that had no common usage in Stevenson's day, it still appeared in Webster's as late as 1890. N. E. Osselton states that "woundy" derives "from the expletive (*Christ's*) *Wounds* . . . [and belongs] to the slangy colloquialism of the post-Restoration writers" (*Branded Words in English Dictionaries before Johnson* [Groningen, 1958], p. 88).

79.31 *Tyrolean*
"Query: Aeolian?" (MS).

81.35 *bum*
Cry; have a habit of weeping (JW).

85.25 *header*
"A plunge head foremost into water . . . a theatrical expression for any supposedly daring jump of hero or heroine in sensational dramas" (JCH).

88.19 *plant*
A hidden store of money or valuables (JCH).

94.6 *clapped down*
Sat down suddenly; crouched; squatted as a hare (JW).

97.1 *sick*
A vulgar expression meaning very indifferent, contemptible (JRB).

98.20 *trick*
Intercourse, dealings; trade, business, traffic (JW).